Magical Midlife Uncorked
The Wine, Chocolate & Paranormal Shenanigans Series
LARISSA EMERALD

Castle Oak Publishing LLC

Magical Midlife Uncorked

The Wine, Chocolate & Paranormal Shenanigans Series, Book 2

Copyright © 2022 by Larissa Emerald

ISBN: 978-1-942139-22-5

ISBN: 978-1-942139-27-0

Castle Oak Publishing LLC

Published in the United States of America

http://www.larissaemerald.com

Follow Larissa Emerald on Facebook

Magical Midlife Uncorked

The Wine, Chocolate, and Paranormal Shenanigans Series

Why now? Because you weren't ready to accept the truth. Weren't ready to let go and accept something else. Sometimes, you have to let go to have something new.

CHAPTER ONE

My Head Hurts

CHOCOLATE. CHOCOLATE. CHOCOLATE. SHE needed to fortify herself for the day ahead.

Lainie Cassidy sank the spoon into the gooey chocolaty dessert, getting just the right-sized bite. She was getting good at conjuring up sweets using the timepiece. She let the bite of chocolate mud pie melt in her mouth. She'd imagined the addition of Bailey's Irish Cream in this concoction. The delightful mixture turned out heavenly. *Mmm.*

She fixed a second cup of coffee before sitting at the island counter, eating another spoonful. Kalen, the dragon-shifter who had been conjured by the timepiece from a romance book she'd been reading, strolled into the kitchen. "Want some?" Lainie asked, pointing her spoon at the dessert.

"It's nine-thirty in the morning," he said.

"Chocolate is a twenty-four-hour affair. Have you learned nothing in the month you've been here?"

"I'm a bacon-and-eggs guy." He opened the freezer, taking out two of the egg, bacon, and cheese muffins she'd bought for him, then put them in the microwave. His coffee was ready in the Keurig, and he added cream and sugar while his breakfast cooked. He'd learned to use some of the electronics around the house: the stove, microwave, toaster, computer, but most of all the TV.

"So why the need for chocolate this early?" Kalen asked. "It can only mean you expect to deal with something bad."

"The fairy Felicity said I should get the box that goes with the timepiece. That means I have to visit the trailer. I plan on sneaking in while John is at work."

"What's the big deal?"

"Well, I haven't been there since I fled John three weeks ago. If he's not there, no problem. If I get caught, could be a big problem." After eating the last bite of chocolaty goodness, she licked the spoon.

"Hmm, I see."

She was sure he didn't. John was an abusive SOB. If he caught her, it wouldn't go well for her. Leaving him and taking the kids with her had taken all the courage she could muster. It had been a godsend when she'd discovered the magical timepiece her grandmother had left her. Facing John now, that was her worst fear. Well, maybe she placed it second to falling on her face trying to make it on her own.

"Do you want me to go with you?"

"No. I can do this. It won't take me long." She stood, tucking the timepiece into her purse.

As she slipped the timepiece into her purse, a faint vibration fluttered beneath her fingers—like the feeling of realizing someone was standing behind her when no one was there. Lainie stilled. The sensation vanished as quickly as it came, leaving only a whisper of pressure in the air around her. She shook her head. Nerves. Wine. Stress. But something inside her—a quiet, instinctive part she'd long ignored—told her the timepiece wasn't reacting to *her*. It was reacting to something... else.

Breathing deeply, she straightened, preparing for the task ahead. Just in case, she jotted down a name and phone number on a little notepad. "If I don't return by two o'clock, call my sister, Crystal."

The coast was clear.

Lainie craned her neck to make sure John's truck wasn't parked in the driveway before she turned off the road. She wasn't concerned anyone else would see her because the property was well hidden by shrubbery. A weight built in her gut as she parked the van within a few yards of the trailer, leaving the engine running. This wouldn't take long. Her heart bounced with anxiety. At ten-thirty in the morning, John should be at work.

He hadn't left a message on her phone in a week. Her lawyer said the divorce would be final in a few days. Maybe that was why. Felicity had said she needed to get the box that went with the pocket watch. So here she was, breaking into the trailer... Well, not really. She was still legally married to John, and technically, half the stuff inside was hers, but that was a moot point.

Felicity, the fairy who had materialized out of the timepiece, had given her a warning about other supernatural beings who would be after the watch. Lainie was still trying to sort it all out. Like, for one, fairies were *real*. Who knew? And Sarah, the woman Lainie had met at the pawn shop when she'd thought of trading the pocket watch for money, well, she was a witch—one who had already tried to steal it.

Anyway, she needed to get the box from the trailer to pair it with the timepiece. And she didn't dare ask her ex because she couldn't take to risk of him smashing it or hiding it from her.

What she needed wouldn't take long to find.

The pocket watch's decorative box should be in the back of the closet where she'd left it.

She hoped her soon-to-be ex hadn't paid attention to what she'd left behind other than the box of knickknacks from the China cabinets that he'd delivered to her. She'd thought he was being nice. At the same time, she'd wondered what he wanted from her. He was rarely agreeable. She was waiting for the other shoe to drop.

It had only been two weeks since she'd fled the home she'd lived in for eighteen years—such a short time after escaping her abusive husband. So much had changed.

Felicity had told her that she had magic capable of directing the power of the timepiece. But that she also needed the box that went with the timepiece. That meant she had to get the box from the trailer.

Her stomach tightened as she hurried up the steps to the trailer, then inserted the key into the lock. Would he have gone to the trouble of changing the locks? With a twist of the key, the door opened. Nope. Either he didn't care if she returned, or he hadn't anticipated that she would.

Lainie ducked inside. She moved quickly because she wanted to get out of there. Too many bad memories plagued her, making her heart beat faster and her hands tremble.

John hadn't done much cleaning. Dirty dishes filled the sink, and clothes were draped over the sofa. Lainie sprinted to the bedroom, anticipating grabbing the box and getting out of there. Hopefully, matching the timepiece with the box would complete the puzzle of the watch and give her the information she needed to control the magic.

She stopped abruptly when she saw the opened closet and a pile of things sitting in the corner. Goosebumps bristled along her arms. He must have gone through it.

She knelt to inspect the closet, reaching toward the back where she'd left the box. Frantically, she patted around in the dark space.

Her hand struck empty shoe boxes, but nothing that felt like the hard wooden container. Her heart sank. It wasn't there.

She sat back on her heels. *Darn it, John. What did you do with it?*

She fixed her attention on the pile in the corner, then rummaged through it. It contained clothes she had decided to leave behind and the shoebox of high-school mementos. Even though those memories tempted her, she focused on the task at hand, and left it there. Standing, she put her hands on her hips and looked around.

Pent-up air whooshed through her lips. She scanned the room. There was a stack of John's clothes on the chair in the corner. The bathroom was beyond that. She turned her attention back into the room. Relief filled her when she spotted the box sitting on John's dresser.

Lainie almost ran to the dresser and picked it up. Something rattled inside as the tipped it. When she opened it, it was full of coins. John must have found the box when he'd rummaged through the closet and liked it enough to put it to use.

She dumped the coins onto his dresser, wishing he hadn't found it. Now, when he noticed it missing, he'd realize she had been there.

That would likely become a problem. But it couldn't be helped. She needed the box to go with the timepiece. That had been her mission.

She stepped back, wondering why she felt such pain about returning here.

Because your biggest, deepest wish is to be loved for who you are. Scars and all, her inner voice said. And she hadn't found that with John. Now, she feared she'd never be enough for anyone.

The house phone rang and she jumped. Her heart thumped wildly in her ears. It went to voicemail. John's recorded message echoed out of the phone base. "Hey, babe. Sorry about this morning. I'll be home for lunch. We can talk about the cruise then."

Every muscle in her body tensed. Who was the message for? A female? She'd been here this morning? Shit. It was a wonder she hadn't run into her. Or maybe she'd be back any moment.

Lainie hustled back through the living room. There were other belongings she'd left behind, but she decided none of it mattered anymore. Besides, she didn't want to spend the time collecting them. It was bad enough John would discover that the box was missing and know she'd been in the house. Turning, she headed out, locking the door behind her.

She climbed into the van, its engine still running, and set the decorative box and her purse in the passenger seat. With her luck, John would pull in the drive at any moment. Or the bimbo the message had been for. He seemed to have a sixth sense with the ability to catch her in the worst moments. That had changed with her discovery of the magical timepiece Nana had given her. Due to its magic, she'd had begun to acquire a number of things she hadn't expected: money, fun things like yummy desserts, Sawyer, a cat that talked, Kalen, a hunky guy out of a romance book who was also a dragon shifter, and Felicity, a magical fairy who was very bossy.

And as for John, she'd gained some power over John, seeming to make him more agreeable. At least that was how it seemed. Although, knowing her soon-to-be ex, that didn't seem possible.

Most of the offerings were totally weird, but the last— She'd take that change any day of the week.

A car horn blew somewhere in the distance, and she stiffened, turning to stare toward the street. As she backed the van out into the road, her heart pattered wildly in her chest.

It wasn't John. Keep going.

Her body didn't relax until she was back on the road, driving away from the trailer. She caught herself speeding and slowed, sinking her spine into the seat with a sigh. Her gaze swept the area to make sure there weren't any police nearby. A sheriff's car passed her coming from the opposite direction. That was too close. It wouldn't do to get a ticket.

For some reason, she didn't feel safe until she reached the rental home. The rustic, orange two-story with its teal shutters was a welcome sight, even if she still wasn't accustomed to the vibrant color choice. She parked in the garage and closed the door. Shutting herself in made her feel a little better. She liked the notion of shutting out the rest of the world. After a quiet moment and a deep breath, she picked up the box and her purse and headed inside.

Mission accomplished.

She set the decorative box on the counter in the kitchen, then removed the timepiece from her purse and set it beside the box.

Her nerves were stretched taught, and she felt weak as if exerting a lot of energy. Hot flash. She needed something sugary to replace the energy she'd expelled.

She opened the refrigerator. Her gaze settled on the leftover chocolate brownies. That would do.

Footsteps pattered in the stairwell. Lainie peered around the door of the fridge as Kalen came into the kitchen. Sawyer trotted beside him.

"Hello," Kalen said, lifting his chin toward the counter. "You found the box. That's excellent."

"Yes. I'm lucky. John had found it, but he'd kept it on his dresser to hold change and knickknacks." She took out the plate of brownies. "I'm having a sugar fix. Would you like a brownie?"

"Yes, please," Kalen said.

"Give me a small piece as well," Sawyer added.

"I don't want you to get sick," she said to the cat.

"No worries. I'm not your typical cat. Right?"

"True." She slid plates of brownies onto the counter along with forks for herself and Kalen, and a small piece for Sawyer. She sat in the chair next to Kalen, cutting off a bite of chocolaty goodness and eating it. Mmm. She closed her eyes as the familiar sweet treat caused her whole body to chill out and unwind. She moaned.

"That good, huh?" Sawyer said.

She opened her eyes to find Kalen staring at her; his gaze seemed to hide wicked thoughts. Lainie looked away.

The cat nibbled at his piece. He was an unusual cat who ate too much human food. Lainie wondered about that. Was it due to his ability to talk that he seemed so humanlike?

She drew the decorative box closer to her so she could study it while she finished eating. "Well, do you two have knowledge about the timepiece or not? And if so, why aren't you telling me?"

Kalen eyed Sawyer. The cat licked his paw, then smoothed it over an ear.

"We only get knowledge on a need-to-know basis," Kalen said. "I haven't the slightest idea of the secrets it holds. Magic is secretive and tricky. And it always comes at a price."

"Oh great. That helps a lot," she said sarcastically. "What about you, cat? Have anything to add to that?" Lainie asked.

"Nope. What he said."

Although she'd noted the complexity of the box when she'd first found it in the closet, she hadn't given it much attention, focusing more on the intricacy of the pocket watch. The inlay on the lid seemed to be made up of a mix of metals, silver, copper, maybe a touch of gold. The Celtic knot comprised the center. She traced the designs with the pad of her fingertip. In the upper left corner was a dragonfly.

She thought of the dragonflies and frogs that had been running loose in her house last week.

On her phone, Lainie did a Google search for dragonflies. "Hmm."

"What do you see?" Kalen asked.

She tilted her phone so he could see the picture. Given that he'd been conjured from a paranormal romance novel, he didn't understand today's technology. "The internet is like a book of information, only it's much easier to find things on it."

"And about dragonflies?"

"Well, they're the fast insect. They can fly up to speeds of thirty-five miles per hour. They can even fly in reverse."

"Huh."

"To some people, they represent renewal and rebirth. And this is interesting, some say they can travel between dimensions, connecting with fairies and the realms of other magical creatures." She paused. "We do have our timepiece fairy. Maybe there was a connection, after all."

"Okay. What else?" Sawyer asked.

"The top right corner has a butterfly," she said. "I think butterflies also mean transformation. Let's see." She typed in the Google search.

"And for the butterfly?" Kalen asked.

"It means rebirth as well, brings color and joy, embracing a new path, the power of air, attraction toward light." Lainie peered at the butterfly on the lid. Was she the butterfly, going through a rebirth into a new life without John? She hoped there was joy in that life ahead of her.

"The bumble bee next," Kalen said.

Lainie changed her search again. "The bee is a sign of courage, winged messengers between worlds, and community."

"And now for the dragon," Lainie said looking at Kalen. "The dragon is foremost known for protection, and an ally against dangerous foe. Associated with courage, wisdom, power, and a gatekeeper and guardian of secrets."

"And the knot in the center means it has no beginning and no end," Sawyer contributed.

"Yes. There are all kinds of Celtic knots. This one looks like a Dara knot. The Celtic symbol for strength." She tilted her phone so they could see the example she'd found.

"Okay. So that's the outside of the box. There must be something more. The fairy Felicity seemed adamant that you get the box." Sawyer sat on the counter beside where Kalen leaned on his elbow.

Lainie opened the lid and peered inside. As she did, her shoulder brushed against Kalen's arm. It made her feel very aware of his size and strength, and that he also changed into a dragon.

She swallowed back her sudden set of nerves. "I don't see anything inside." She tilted it backward to examine the underside of the lid. A glimpse of metal flashed, catching the light of the overhead can lights in the ceiling. "There's something on the lid."

She tilted the box back further and pulled it closer at the same time. "It looks like the lid is lined with a plate. It must be silver and tarnished. I'll look for some cleaner."

Lainie rummaged beneath the sink to find a cleaner that would work on metals. She found Brasso in a little yellow bottle and Weiman silver wipes. She chose the wipes.

Back at the counter, she plucked a wipe from the canister and carefully wiped over the plate in the lid. The dark tarnish changed to shiny silver as she swiped across it. When it was clean, she could make out letters imprinted in the metal. It used the English alphabet, but the words weren't in English.

With a frustrated sigh, she sat back on the barstool, thinking. How was this going to help if she couldn't read it. "Is it Gaelic?"

"Yes. It looks like Old Irish Gaelic," Kalen said.

What if a translation program could make it out?

She positioned her phone over the text and snapped a picture. If she couldn't manage the translation on her phone, she could try her computer. Kalen and Sawyer watched intently. The technology still baffled them.

Kalen read the words in his rich Irish-accented voice.

Is ru, a chiall, subsaig gach gniomhair
A sgriohas mi, is tusa brigh gach dain,
Mineachadh gach seantans is gach briarthair.

"You're Irish. Do you know what it says?" Lainie asked Kalen as she got a pen and paper from the desk drawer. Her phone translation app had come up with something. She wrote down the original text, and then translation, word for word.

"Not all of it. That word is *clock*. Time, dream," Kalen said, pointing to individual words. It was a puzzle to decipher. The more words they uncovered, the more it resembled a poem or riddle. It certainly wasn't a clear a, b, c of instructions on how the pocket watch operated.

When she written out the entire translation, Kalen read it aloud.

Thou art the wind and I the lyre:
Strike, O Wind, on the sleeping strings.
Strike till the dead heart stirs and sings!
Pass, O Clock, I make you dream.
Touch of the stones and thrill me deep.

Her heart fluttered as she listened to him.

The timepiece belongs to one owner. That she gathered from what Felicity had said.

Open once, it hears what's on your mind. Touch the stones and the fairy comes.

Hold it from above and spin it like the Earth on its axis.

Lainie looked at Kalen. They'd been working at this for more than an hour and hadn't gotten very far. "We must set this aside for a while," she said.

"You figured out a few pieces. That's a start."

"Yes, but it looks like I'm not going to be able to send you back into the book the way I'd intended. You're gonna have to stay here for an extended period of time. We'll need to go shop for some more clothes for you and perhaps rearrange the office into a bedroom. We should do that while the kids are at school."

"I have clothes," Kalen said. "You already bought me some."

"Those were just a few things to tide you over. I thought I would be sending you back into the book."

Laney got the pitcher of tea from the refrigerator and poured a fresh glass into her Yeti cup. She found a second glass and fixed Kalen a drink also.

"Sawyer, why don't you see if you can make friends with Bitsy? The dog trotted over at the mention of her name.

"Oh, yeah. You guys get to go do the fun shopping and leave me here with the pooch," Sawyer grumbled.

"Kalen, you should put your sandals on. Then we'll go."

Lainie checked the ongoing list on her phone. It seemed to be lacking several items. "I hate it when I remember something, then turn around and forget."

CHAPTER TWO

Did I Do That

LAINIE DASHED UPSTAIRS TO her bedroom closet, opening the duffle bag that held her stash of cash. The magic money kept coming. Every morning since she'd left John, fifty-thousand dollars showed up in her purse. It has been like winning the Publishers Clearing House prize, only this had been conjured by the timepiece.

Unsure how costly it would be to outfit Kalen and buy a bed, she transferred two thousand to her wallet. That would be her limit for today.

Downstairs, she met up with Kalen. "Ready?"

Once Kalen had his sandals on, Lainie led the way out the door into the garage. She pushed the garage door opener on the wall, then the door trundled up. Kalen watched in amazement as it went. It was fun to see him as he observed new and different things.

"Walk around to the other side of the van and get in," Lainie instructed.

Kalen walked around and put his hands on the door. He touched the handle but didn't seem to know how it operated. "You pull up the handle," Lainie said. From the other side of the car, Lainie leaned over and watched him slip his fingers around the handle. He yanked on it. Lainie gave a little screech because she thought he was going to pull the handle off the door. She walked around the van, put her hand in the handle, and demonstrated how it was done. Patiently, she said, "Gently. You don't realize how strong you are."

She opened the door for him. "This is a new car, and I don't want it destroyed. Go ahead and get in."

After he slid into the seat, she grabbed the seat belt from above his shoulders and tugged it down, reaching across him and leaning in. Her breath mingled with his as she found the clasp and pushed the buckle into place. She was surprised by the pleasant sensations she felt at their close proximity.

"This is a seat belt," she explained. "It keeps you safe when you're riding inside the vehicle."

She closed the door, walked back around the van, and got in the driver's side, fastening her own seat belt. He watched. His brows pushed together. His first car ride was going to be interesting. Talk about being over stimulated, she thought. She was curious to see how this trip would go, and a little worried. What if he did something totally inappropriate? She started the car with the push of a button, put it into gear, and backed out of the driveway into the street. As she drove down the street, he pressed his head back against the headrest. As she turned the corner, he grabbed onto the door handle.

His concerned expression was priceless. It amused her. The big, tough knight was almost frozen, totally out of his element.

Lainie pointed out items that would be new to him. "That's a traffic light," she said. "When it's red, it means we have to stop. When it's green, that means that we can go. And then the traffic from the other direction has to stop. That way, we don't have accidents or crashes."

"So many new things," he said. "But I've seen these on the television. So, it's not a complete surprise."

"Yes, I imagine so. But it is probably different in reality," she said.

She thought it would be as hard to go backward in time as it would be to go forward. Especially given all the new technology that was available today. Again, she went to the nearest shopping center. "We'll begin with the clothes first," she said. "Then shoes."

As she turned into the shopping center, he again grabbed the door handle. She parked. "This is a shopping center where we buy clothes. It has multiple stores," she said.

"To get out of the car, you lift this lever," she demonstrated, then let him find it on his door. It wasn't too hard. He found it right away.

He followed her example, exiting the car and closing the door behind him. She pushed the button, automatically locking the van. They heard the click, and he looked over the vehicle at her.

Together, they walked into one of her favorite stores—TJ Maxx. She grabbed a shopping cart along the way, then headed for the men's department. When they got there, they strolled up and down the aisles. It was fun to choose items that she thought would look good on him. He was movie-star handsome, so it wasn't a hardship at all. She selected pairs of jeans again and a few T-shirts.

He riffled through a couple of racks before pulling out some novelty shirts that interested him, one with a race car, another with a grizzly bear, and one with a guy holding a sword. Next, she grabbed him another swimsuit, so she wouldn't find him swimming naked in the pool again. Not that she minded, but she rented in a subdivision of nosy neighbors.

They moved on to the shoe department, picking up some socks along the way.

There, she found a foot-measuring apparatus, making him stand on it to see what size shoe he needed. "You wear size eleven," she said.

Spotting a pair of Nikes with black-and-blue stripes along the sides, she selected a size eleven and then showed him. "Men wear different kinds of shoes. These are called sneakers. They're good for walking and running. Have a seat in that chair so you can try them on."

Opening the box, she took the shoes out and adjusted the shoelaces, then handed him a pair of socks. "Here put these on first. Then the shoes." When she had the laces fixed just right, she knelt on the floor in front of him, then held out one shoe to help him slip it on.

For some reason, it seemed like an intimate task. She blushed as he watched her intently. Once he put his foot into the shoe, she fixed the laces for him and tied them. Then she repeated the process on the other foot.

"How's that?"

"They feel different," Kalen said.

"Bet they do. I'm sure they had nothing like this in your time."

"No, my footwear was made out of leather."

"Walk around a little bit. See how they feel."

Kalen walked several steps down the aisle, then turned around. He jumped, sidestepped, and ran in place.

A woman pushing a stroller walked by, paused, and arched a quizzical brow. Lainie imagined that not very many grown men tested out shoes quite that vigorously.

"Do you like them?" Lainie asked.

"I think they will do," Kalen said. "You're a better judge than I am on what's appropriate." A pair of leather dockers caught his eye. He strolled over, lifted them from the shelf, and examined their structure.

Patiently, she found the appropriate boxes, then ran her finger down them until she found a size eleven, making sure he followed her actions. Thankfully, they had a pair in his size. After, pulling the box from the shelf, she turned to him. "Would you like to try them on?"

His eyes lit up. Apparently, this was something he related to. "Yes."

He returned to the chair where he'd sat earlier. "These shoes can be worn with or without socks. Your choice," she said.

He paused. "Without."

One at a time, she handed them to him. He put them on. They still had laces to tie but only ones that crisscrossed. He seemed to know how to handle that.

"This leather is different from what I'm accustomed to. Softer."

"They have machines that help with the production process, I imagine. That would make them more pliable."

He walked around the shoe department. Up one aisle and down the other. His gait seemed more natural this time.

"They look good on you," she said.

"Thank you. May we purchase these, as well?"

"Of course. You need more than one pair of shoes." Lainie took the shoes from him and added them to the cart.

Kalen crossed his arms, his brows coming together. "It's not right that you should pay for these. I need to work. To pay my own way."

Lainie rested her hand on his arm, leaning close to him, and said quietly, "I'm not paying for them. It's the magic money from the pocket watch."

He nodded. "Perhaps. But I still want to earn my keep." His jaw tightened. "Felicity charged me with protecting you from those who would steal the talisman, aye—but that means more than swinging a sword. We should begin a proper training schedule."

Lainie frowned. "Didn't we already do that?"

"What you've done so far was the first layer," he said. "You know how to call your magic and how to defend yourself in a pinch. Now you must learn how to use it without shouting your presence to every hungry creature within a hundred miles."

A little chill slid down her spine at that.

"We'll talk about it when we get home," she said, but the words didn't feel like avoidance this time. They felt like a promise.

We'll talk about it when we get home." She wasn't ready to admit to being in any real danger. "We'll pay for this, and maybe grab some lunch at Sam's when we look for a mattress." She supposed she could shop at a furniture store for what they needed, but that would mean they'd have to wait to have it delivered. She needed quick and convenient, not fancy. This was a temporary circumstance after all. It was time to get serious about finding her new home.

Lainie and Kalen took their purchases to the check-out counter where a woman with short purple hair rang up the sale. Kalen looked from the young woman to Lainie, obviously concerned by the woman's hair and the tattoos of flowers covering one arm.

The cashier kept slipping glances at him. Kalen had an unmissable presence. He seemed to take up a lot of space simply by standing. Perhaps people sensed the dragon in him. He didn't say a word, but he gave off an aura of power and authority.

Lainie paid cash for the purchase. Kalen hefted four bags, leaving Lainie one. As they exited, she could feel the cashier's gaze following them.

Well, he was younger than she her, she thought, *and hot as sin*. With this being their first time out together, she hadn't thought about how it might look. Not that they were an item, but she had to admit the idea made her feel...young, naughty, and alive.

When they got in the van, she took a long drink from her Yeti, allowing the tea to cool her fiery thoughts. Heat suffused her face, which had nothing to do with the temperature outside.

"Would you like some of your drink?" she asked, reminding him that she'd brought along a drink for him also.

He accepted the drink and stared at the lever. She flipped her finger over the lid, opening it for him. "Ah. I see." He tipped the cup up. "It's a canteen."

She paused at his description. "Yes. I suppose it is."

Lainie drove to their next stop about five miles down the road. Inside Sam's, she led the way to the food counter. She often grabbed a bite to eat when she came here because she could get lunch for under five dollars. Plus, it was convenient. "They have hot dogs, sausages, or pizza. Does any of that interest you?"

He smiled. "Pizza."

It was a novelty for him. "Two meat-lovers slices and two drinks."

"Do they serve wine?"

"No. There is an array of drinks to choose from over there." She pointed over to the drink dispensers. "They don't serve alcoholic beverages."

Lainie paid for their order, and the cashier handed her two cups. She led the way to the drink dispenser. "I'm going to have Coke. It's a soda. They have an assortment of sodas, or you can choose tea, with sugar or without."

She filled her disposable cup with ice and held it beneath the dispenser, tapping the appropriate flavor. The soda sprayed into the cup with a whoosh.

"I will also try Coke."

She raised a brow. So far, since he'd appeared at her house, he'd only had water and wine. She wondered what he'd think of the carbonated drink.

They sat at a table. "Your pizza is ready," the cashier said.

Kalen watched as other customers approached the counter and ordered. Lainie got their pizza slices, then set the paper plates on the table along with some napkins. They ate in silence. At least he was familiar with pizza since they'd had it at home. When he drank the soda, his face scrunched, and he tilted his head to the side. "The fizz went up my nose," he announced.

"I guess it can do that. I'd forgotten."

"It's sweet."

"Soda has a lot of sugar."

After he took another sip, he made the same face but recovered quickly. "I'm not sure I like Coke."

"It grows on you," Lainie explained.

He lifted a doubtful brow.

"So, here's the plan. When the kids get home from school, I'm going to introduce you as a renter of the extra room. I can't keep hiding you away. You're the brother of a friend of mine in the dance community. And you're new in town, visiting from Ireland to see if you can move here. That means no job yet."

He nodded. "You're good at this."

She flashed a smile. "What kind of job would you be looking for? What did you do in Ireland?"

He snickered. "I was a Provincial Inspector in the Irish Constabulary."

"A policeman?"

"Aye. Large families usually had one son stay on the farm, another join the church, and one enlist in law enforcement or military service." He shrugged. "I wasn't about to join the church."

"Well, that won't work for getting a job here." She angled her head, studying him. "Maybe you could be looking for a security-guard position or private investigator. A bit James Bond-ish."

"Who? What's that?"

"Never mind. We can watch one of his movies on television later. Actually, you look more like Liam Neeson." She finished the last of her pizza. "The main thing is we need to get our story straight about what we tell my kids." She slurped the last of her soda through the straw. "I mean, introducing you as a guy conjured from my romance book by a magical timepiece isn't going to cut it."

She really needed to carve out more reading time to discover more about him.

Kalen stared at her, perplexed, as he popped the last bite of pizza in his mouth and took one last sip of his drink before tossing the remainder in the trash.

Lainie glanced around, noticing a short man stepping out from behind the vitamin aisle, but when he caught sight of Lainie, he hopped back and out of sight. She squinted at his odd behavior. It was as if she'd caught him spying on them. She shrugged it off.

Lainie grabbed a shopping cart and led the way to the furniture aisle. She selected a ticket for a queen mattress set, plus the metal frame. Then she selected bed linens, sheets, pillows, and a bedspread set that she placed in the cart. "That will do it for this trip," she said. "I'll show this to the cashier, and they will deliver the bed out front. We'll have help tying it onto the roof of the van. The drive home is short, so we shouldn't have any problems."

"If you say so," Kalen said.

Yeah, he wouldn't know one way or the other about the challenges of driving with a mattress and box spring atop your car.

Lainie swung by the meats section and grabbed precooked spareribs, a few bags of vegetables, and baking potatoes for dinner. Again, she spotted the man from earlier, still staring at her. She'd been in stores before where it seemed like she passed the same people repeatedly. But this seemed different. Each time she saw the guy, he appeared guilty and evasive.

At the checkout counter, the cashier totaled the bill and ordered the mattress, box springs, and frame to be delivered out front. Lainie paid and pushed the cart of bedding outside. "Wait here. I'm going to drive the van up."

She left him on the walkway, holding the cart. Lainie got the van and circled the parking lot so she could enter the pick-up lane. Blushing, she smiled when the store associate came out with the bed and eyed Kalen.

Kalen sidestepped the people exiting the store, saying to one woman, "I'm sorry. I'm waiting for someone to deliver my bed." She shot a glance between Lainie and Kalen. She had no way of knowing their circumstances, of course, but Lainie's mind went in a direction of its own, putting her in bed with him.

Wrong.

Lainie put the bed frame, linens, and food items in the back of the van. Two store workers hoisted the bed set onto the roof of the van and secured them with rope ties. "Thank you for your help," she said to them both.

"That should get you home all right," one worker said.

There the man was again. What was with this guy? He stood just inside the automatic doors. Her eyes met his. He didn't have any shopping items. She started toward him. He turned and fled.

Kalen followed her attentive gaze. "Is something wrong?"

"I don't know. This is the third time I've found that man watching us. There's something weird about him."

"Weird?"

"Yeah. Strange. Creepy."

"Hmm. Maybe he's after your magic." He said it with a teasing smile, but the look he shot toward the man was anything but amused.

His words hit Lainie like a gut punch. "Felicity did say creatures would be after the timepiece." Saying it out loud made the air feel thicker.

"I know." Kalen's expression hardened. "I just didn't expect them to come sniffing around your grocery runs quite so soon."

He watched the automatic doors slide shut behind the man. "This is what I meant about training," he added quietly. "It's not enough to know how to throw power around. You have to learn how to move in a world where something like that—" he jerked his chin toward the store "—can track you by what it feels when you use the watch."

"No pressure," she muttered.

"On the contrary," he said. "There is great pressure. That's why we'll start as soon as we're home."

Lainie drove cautiously home, taking extra care on the corners. Pulling into the driveway, she stopped, opening the garage. "With the added height of the stuff on top, I don't think we will clear the garage. We can take them in from here. I'm going to put the grocery items in the fridge, and I'll be right back."

Both Kalen and Lainie got out of the van. She took the grocery bags in through the garage.

"Undo the ropes, and we'll carry it in together," she said when she came back.

Kalen followed her instructions. With the ties undone, the box spring came down first. They turned it on its edge. "We'll take it through the front door. It's the most direct route."

Kalen was strong. His biceps bulged as he took the brunt of the weight. It surprised Lainie how little of the load she had to bear. When they reached the door, she paused to press the code to unlock it. Then, they finagled the box spring through the door and propped it against the inside wall.

"Help me rearrange the furniture in the office, please," Lainie said.

They pushed the small desk and chair against the wall, freeing the space where the bed would go. Next, they brought in the bedframe and set it up. The box spring went on top of that. Then, they brought in the mattress. Lainie set aside the bedspread, pillows, and shams, then tossed the sheets in the washing machine.

She wasn't one to usually perspire a lot, but after that bit of exertion, she was dripping from head to toe. She shook her head. What was with that? Grabbing a handful of paper towels, she dampened them and dabbed her face and neck with the cool water, then went into the living room and collapsed on the sofa.

"Okay, can you fetch the bags of your new clothes from the car?" She checked the time on her phone. "The kids will be home from school in thirty minutes."

Lainie heard the front door open and close. She must have dosed off while he brought his shopping bags in and put them away. The next thing she knew, Bitsy jumped onto her lap, startling her awake. There was noise in the kitchen, someone shuffling around. Then Kalen appeared, holding out a glass of wine. She tilted her head back, looking at his handsome face. His dark brown eyes twinkled, and his mouth broke into a lazy smile.

"Here, I thought you could use this," he said.

"Oh, you sweet, sweet man." She sighed, accepting the glass. He had one as well. She enjoyed a long sip, swept her tongue across her lips, and smiled. "Mmm, just what I needed. Thank you."

"Nae problem." He sank into the chair adjacent to her.

She offered her glass, touching his in a gentle clink. "To new adventures," she said, then added under her breath, "preferably the kind I'm prepared for."

Kalen's smile turned knowing. "Then we had best make sure your training keeps up, lass."

"Cheers," he said and drank.

"I think you've been learning stuff from watching TV."

"Perhaps. However, I was conjured out of a romance novel. I do know how to treat a lady."

Lainie chuckled, somewhat jealous of the heroine in that book. But then again, she had a living, breathing, genuine article sharing wine with her.

When she heard her son's car pull into the driveway, she groaned. The kids were home from school. She downed the rest of her wine, hoping the next twenty minutes would go well.

CHAPTER THREE

Save Your Energy

LAINIE PINCHED THE BRIDGE of her nose, reining in her unease. How would the kids take the idea of a strange man living in the house with them? She rose. Kalen started to stand, but she stopped him with an outstretched hand. "No. Stay put. I'll introduce you to the kids when they come in."

She strolled into the kitchen, setting her empty glass in the sink, ready to greet them. Sawyer took his usual position on the barstool. He had gotten the hang of keeping his mouth shut when the kids were around.

Brennon came in first. "Hey, you left the van in the driveway. How come?"

"Hello to you, too," Lainie said.

Jenna slipped in right behind him.

"I had some large items from the store that I couldn't fit in the garage."

Both kids made their way to the kitchen island, then stared into the living room as they dropped their bookbags on the barstools.

"Guys, this is Kalen McCarthy. He's the brother of one of my dance friends, and he's going to rent a room from us for a while. Kalen, meet my son, Brennon, and my daughter, Jenna."

For half a minute, both kids looked between her and Kalen with their mouths open. Brennon recovered first. "Um, pleased to meet you." He crossed the distance to the living room, offering Kalen his hand. "It will be nice to have a guy around. I'm sort of outnumbered." He chuckled, glancing back at Lainie and Jenna.

Jenna stayed put but waved. "Hi. Nice to meet you."

"I'm pleased to meet you both," Kalen said, his Irish accent clear.

Brennon raised a brow. "Where are you from?"

"Galway. Ireland."

"Wow. You're a long way from home."

"That I am."

Lainie realized it wasn't a good idea to let them ask too many questions. What if her son asked about Kalen's flight or something like that? The dragon shifter wouldn't know how to answer. Could dragons fly across the ocean in their dragon form? She wasn't even sure if shifters could fly in an airplane. What if they shifted during the flight? That wouldn't be good.

"Okay, we picked up a mattress today at Sam's and rearranged the office. There's a full bath downstairs due to the pool, so Kalen can use that. It should be fine." She avoided adding anything about helping with the rent or such. Her kids weren't privy to their finances.

"You're the boss," Brennon said.

She nodded. "Yes, I am." She wanted to add for them to be on their best behavior, but she bit her tongue. A wave of guilt washed through her at making up this story to tell the kids. She didn't know how long she could keep her magical ability from them. Between the separation, the move, and ultimately, the divorce, they had enough to deal with. She didn't want to add to their worries. And Brennon was certainly a worrier.

"Well, I picked up ribs for dinner. I'll put the potatoes in the oven, toss together a salad, and we'll eat in about an hour. That sound all right?"

"That's good. I'm starved," Brennon said as he took a soda from the fridge.

Jenna was right behind him, doing the same. Then they both grabbed their school bags and froze as Chinchy scampered out of Kalen's room into the living room.

"What...what is that?" Jenna scooted sideways, knocking shoulders with Brennon.

"A guinea pig?" Brennon asked.

"She's a chinchilla. Kalen's pet. She'll be staying in his room," Lainie explained.

Brennon followed the animal into the living room, pausing and bending, making kissy sounds. "What's its name?"

"Chinchy," Kalen said.

"Come here, Chinchy," Brennon called.

Lainie wasn't surprised at all when the chinchilla crawled into Brennon's open hand. Standing, he stroked her, tucking the little critter close to his chest. "She's super soft. You should feel her, Jenna."

"Nope. I'm good."

Brennon cuddled Chinchy for a few minutes then handed her to Kalen. "She's cute."

"Thanks," Kalen said, allowing the chinchilla to run up his arm where she perched on his shoulder.

Brennon met up with Jenna, and they both went up to their rooms. "I don't think they bite," Laine heard him say to his sister.

Lainie leaned her hip against the counter, staring after them for a minute. She was incredibly proud of them. Maybe it had been living through all the difficult times with John that now allowed them to go with the flow. Walking on eggshells throughout their childhood couldn't have been easy. But they'd all survived, not unscathed, but stronger for it.

"You can turn the TV on if you'd like," she told Kalen. He found the remote, then tapped the buttons. One thing he'd learned to do in the short time he'd been here was how to work the TV.

"That went better than I expected," Sawyer said.

"Yes. It did. I'm thankful."

She poured another glass of wine to sip while she prepared dinner. After she scrubbed the potatoes, she put them in the oven to bake. The salad came already prepared in a bag, so all she did was rinse it, then add tomatoes and cucumbers. She wrapped the ribs in foil, then added those to the oven. They may have been better if she'd done them on the grill, but she wasn't in the mood to deal with the cleanup.

The one thing she hadn't bought was dessert, but there were plenty of yummy things to try in the dessert magazine she'd gotten. Hopefully, she could find something quick, easy, and that she had all the ingredients for. Then again, perhaps it didn't matter if she made it with magic. After retrieving the magazine from the desk in the corner, she thumbed through the pages.

The timepiece had produced delicious desserts before—with Felicity hovering nearby like a magical safety net. Could she replicate it now? On demand? With intention and without supervision?

A chocolate cheesecake caught her eye. She spread the magazine on the counter, the recipe open.

Usually, when she conjured things, she'd relied on the "touch the book and hope" method. Maybe that had been the beginner's version of using the talisman. Felicity kept saying she could learn to *shape* the magic instead of just triggering it.

She took the watch from her purse, studying the familiar swirl of metal. In the past, she'd just set it on the page and waited. Tonight, she wanted to see what happened if *she* did more of the work. Cocking her head, she listened—muffled thumps and voices drifted down from the game room. Good. The kids were distracted. No witnesses if this went sideways.

"You're really going to do the deed," Sawyer remarked.

She nodded. "Felicity keeps telling me I have to practice while things are quiet. This counts as quiet."

She opened the watch and held it out at arm's length toward the picture of the cheesecake. Drawing a steady breath, she focused on the image—texture, shine, the way the chocolate would give under a fork.

Anticipation rolled through her as a sharp, bright current gathered in her chest and streamed down her arm to the timepiece. It felt like the watch wasn't separate from her anymore but an extra joint at the end of her limb, answering her intent.

The power surged harder than she expected. Her breathing quickened, and she had to consciously keep her hand from shaking. "Easy," she whispered to herself, forcing her jaw to unclench. "Don't blow out the circuits."

A cloud of mist swirled over the counter. The pressure in her chest eased, the intensity fading into a light, fizzy tingling beneath her skin. When the mist thinned, a chocolate cheesecake sat exactly where she'd pictured it—rich, glossy, undeniably real.

"You did it," Sawyer said, sounding somewhat surprised.

Lainie blinked. "I did." She felt jubilant and shocked at the same time—right up until a faint throb nudged behind her eyes, like she'd stood up too fast after a long sit. Not awful. Just a clear reminder that magic wasn't free.

Kalen must have heard them. He strolled into the kitchen. "What? You used the timepiece?"

"I did. And I didn't burn the house down. I mean, nothing bad happened. Isn't that great?"

"Yes. Congratulations," Kalen said.

"Thanks." She smiled. How could this have happened? Why could she wield magic? But the evidence was right in front of her. And she couldn't deny the onslaught of power that left her yearning for more. But now wasn't the time to explore those feelings.

The timer on the oven rang. Lainie turned it off, then set the table. She called to the kids, "Dinner."

With this being the first time Kalen had joined them, dinner felt awkward. They served their plates buffet style. Kalen waited to go last even though she'd urged him in front of her. She grabbed extra napkins because ribs were a messy affair. Brennon and Jenna sat on one side of the table while she and Kalen took the seats across from them.

She passed the fixings for a loaded baked potato: butter, bacon bits, sour cream, and shredded cheese. Kalen watched everyone prepare their potato as they liked it. Only then did he follow suit. The same went for the salad, with a choice of salad dressings. He didn't say anything, but she knew this was a first for him.

Brennon watched as Kalen ate with his fork in his left hand, the way most Europeans did.

"Everything tastes delicious. Thank you," Kalen said.

"You're welcome."

She grinned at the kids, "We have a chocolate cheesecake for dessert."

Jenna's eyes lit up. "And we have chocolate syrup in the fridge. I saw it there yesterday."

"That's right. We do." Lainie leaned back in her chair, relaxing. "Thanksgiving is next week. We'll be going to Gramma and Grampa's for dinner. Do you want to stay the weekend afterward with them this year, like you usually do?"

"What about Dad?" Jenna asked.

"Well, he'll be doing his own thing this year."

Brennon and Jenna exchanged a glance. She could tell this was difficult for them, and her heart ached to ease these trying times. "I don't think your dad ever really liked spending holidays with my parents. I grew up in a large family, so I'm used to all the craziness. I love it. But your dad, was an only child. He wasn't used to having a loud, boisterous family." She refrained from adding *unless it was his beer buddies. Then* it was all right.

Brennon spoke first, as he usually did. "I think I'd like to stay at gramma and grampa's like we usually do. They always take us to the beach, and that's fun. Or fishing. Besides, I'll be going to college next year. It may not be the same after that."

He peered at Jenna. "What do you think, Jen?"

"I'm good with that," she answered.

Lainie nodded, preening at Brennon's wise decision. As people got older, who knew how many birthdays they would have left? One day, she knew these moments would matter to the kids because memories would be all they had left.

"Okay. I'll let them know tomorrow so they can plan accordingly," Lainie said.

"What about you, Kalen? Are you coming to Thanksgiving with us?" Jenna asked.

Blankly, he looked stared at Lainie. "He most certainly can if he wants to. We haven't talked about it yet. Gramma's philosophy is *the more the merrier*." Lainie wondered if Kalen even knew what the American holiday was. "Since he's from Ireland, I'm not sure if they celebrate Thanksgiving as we do here."

Looking to Kalen, she explained, "It's a holiday in America where we give thanks for the blessings of the past year."

"I'm fine with whatever you think best," he said to Lainie.

"Good. Then I'll let my mom know you're coming."

He nodded. "All right."

"Who's ready for dessert?" Lainie asked, clearing the plates.

"I am." Jenna rose to help clear the table.

Lainie retrieved the chocolate cheesecake from the refrigerator, sliced it, and served everyone a plated piece, setting the chocolate syrup on the table so they could help themselves. It occurred to her that they'd probably eaten more sweets since moving here than they'd had in ages. It was as if this was an introduction to a better life—one where things were pleasant and wonderful. She pushed the warning from Felicity to the back of her mind.

The chocolate cheesecake was delicious: smooth, creamy, and perfect with a drizzle of syrup on top. She was going to have to join an exercise club if she kept this up.

"Mmm," Kalen said, licking a smear of chocolate off his lips. "This is tasty."

"Yeah. I know," Lainie agreed. "So tomorrow night is the Homecoming dance. Did you order Jade a corsage?"

"Yes. I have to pick it up tomorrow afternoon."

"Sounds good." Lainie hesitated. "Listen, if you'd like, you can drive my van to the dance."

His brows shot up, and he grinned from ear to ear. "Really? That would be awesome."

"Just be home by midnight, or it will turn into a pumpkin."

They all laughed. The slightest hint of unease laced through Lainie. Perhaps she shouldn't joke like that, knowing the timepiece might take her seriously. "Just kidding," she added for good measure.

Brennon gave her an odd look, one that conveyed his *duh, Mom*, without him having to speak.

Jenna gathered the dessert plates from the table. "Mom, Sela asked if I could spend the night at her place tomorrow night. I'd really like to get together with my friends more. It's been three weeks since we left home. I think we're ready to move on."

Lainie eyed her daughter. Jenna was right—they needed to enjoy life. Lainie knew Sela's parents, although not well. "Okay. Let me know the details. Do I need to drop you at her house, or will she be picking you up?"

Jenna beamed. "I'll check on that after I confirm with Sela." She skipped off upstairs.

"I'm heading up, too. Going to practice some shots in the game room," Brennon said.

The patter of feet sounded as he followed Jenna. Lainie rose from the table, then breezed into the kitchen. For some reason, she had energy tonight. It didn't take long to clean the kitchen.

Kalen ambled over to the counter. "I think we should begin your training."

"What do you have in mind?"

"Not just what you've done before." He glanced toward the front of the house, as if seeing threats she couldn't yet. "You've had your first lessons in bearing a blade and calling the watch's power. Now you need to learn how to fight without wasting strength—or broadcasting magic like a beacon."

"I've always wanted to take a self-defense class," she said, thinking of John, of every time she'd wished she'd known even one good move. "If I know a few techniques, I'll feel better about...well, everything."

"This will be more than a few techniques," he said, but his eyes softened. "I'll fetch us a pair of blades."

"Wait. I'll fix Sawyer's and Chinchy's dinners, and you can take them with you."

After she prepared their dishes, she handed them to Kalen.

"Thank you," he said before disappearing toward the stairs.

On the back of the couch where he lounged, the cat stood and stretched. "Hey. I'm over here," he said.

"You usually eat in my room. It won't hurt you to make the trip," Lainie said.

"Right. Which is why you're not hoofing it up there," Sawyer complained.

"Either you want to eat, or you don't." Lainie grinned. She'd raised two children; one dramatic cat didn't intimidate her.

Kalen returned with a sword in each hand. Felicity had magically provided them when she'd appeared with her warning, leaving them with half a dozen weapons.

"Did you choose the largest two to begin training with?" she asked. They looked like the kind of blades King Arthur might've practiced with.

"Each sword has a sheath," Kalen said. "We'll leave it on to practice. It dulls the edge and your chances of accidentally skewering something that shouldn't be skewered. Don't let that make you careless—the weight will still bruise if you're struck."

"Comforting," she muttered. The sheath made the blade feel heavier and more unwieldy.

She glanced around the house, mentally measuring distances, corners, and breakables. The foyer entrance appeared to be the best choice—spacious and mostly void of furniture.

Kalen handed her the slightly shorter sword. As she took it, her arm dipped under the weight. She readjusted her grip, more mindful this time than the first day he'd put a practice blade in her hand.

"Huh," she said, testing a small swing. "Still about as heavy as a gallon of milk. Maybe a gallon and a half."

His mouth curled. "And you're not meant to be hurling milk jugs about in a battle. The goal is not to prove how much you can lift, lass. It's to end the fight before your arms give out."

"So much for my dream of having toned arms as a bonus."

"You'll have those," he said dryly. "But you'll also have breath control, footwork, and the sense to know when not to attack."

She lifted her brows. "I thought the whole point of a sword was attacking."

"The point of surviving," he corrected, "is using as little energy as possible to do what must be done. Save your strength for when you truly need it—for your children, for magic, for the moments when the Collector pushes back. Sword work is a tool, not your entire war."

He stepped into the open space and raised his blade. "You remember the basics from before—overhead strikes, cutting arcs."

She nodded. "My shoulders remember, too. They filed a complaint."

"Tonight we refine," he said. "Fewer big, showy swings. More clean lines. Think of dance—not the spins, but the intent behind where you place your feet."

That, at least, made sense.

"First," he said, "show me an overhead strike the way you've been doing it."

She took a stance and lifted the sword. The motion felt familiar in her muscles now—straight up, then down with a step forward.

Kalen watched her complete the move, then shook his head slightly. "Too much arc. You're painting the air. Shorten it. Bring the blade only as high as needed to clear the block, then down. Again."

She tried it his way—tighter, smaller, less theatrical.

"Better," he said. "You just saved yourself half a breath and a heartbeat. Those add up."

He moved on. "Now, the cut-across you learned. Show me."

She performed the diagonal slice, feeling the pull in her shoulders and back.

"You're overcommitting," he said. He set his sword down and stepped behind her. "Turn sideways to your opponent." His hands closed over her wrists, firm but careful. Heat from his chest radiated across her back, distracting enough that she had to drag her focus back to the lesson.

"Start with the blade horizontal, not towering over your head. Bend your knees. Twist and step forward together—let your legs do the work, not your arms."

Guided by his hands, she tried the move again. It felt completely different—less like chopping wood, more like letting her body carry the blade where it needed to go.

"Good," he said, stepping away. "Now the return cut. If you've committed to one direction, you must know how to come back without losing your balance. Forward angle, then backhand."

He demonstrated, his sword moving in a tight X that wasted no motion at all.

She followed, mimicking his stance, his timing.

"Angle, slice. Backhand cut. Again."

He drilled her through the sequence until her legs burned more than her arms. Her dancer's mind couldn't help clocking the rhythm—step, twist, cut, recover.

"Last one for tonight," he said. "The thrust. Same stance, but keep the blade level. Let your back leg push you forward."

It looked easy when he did it. It was not easy when she tried. Keeping the blade from dipping felt like a battle with gravity itself. Twice she overbalanced and had to catch herself.

"You're fighting the weight," he said. "Stop. Let it settle into your arm. You're not flinging it—you're guiding it."

After several more tries, she managed one thrust that felt clean.

"There," he said. "That's enough."

"I can keep going," she lied. Her thin shirt clung to her skin, sweat cooling in the air-conditioned foyer. Her arms trembled faintly when she tried to lower the sword.

"And you'll be useless tomorrow if you do," he countered. "You have children to care for, a home to run, and magic to practice. Save your energy, Lainie. Overtraining is as dangerous as not training at all."

She let the tip of the blade rest against the floor. "My muscles would like to subscribe to that philosophy."

"Good." His gaze swept over her, not in a way that made her feel self-conscious, but assessing, making sure she truly was all right. "We'll build in layers. Short, frequent practices. Strength and control together. No sense in having a sharp sword if your arms give out before the fight ends."

"You make an excellent case for bubble baths instead," she muttered.

The corner of his mouth lifted. "The pool will do for tonight."

After about forty-five minutes, she was done. Thoroughly. She suspected she'd pay in sore muscles tomorrow, but at least now she knew she hadn't just been flailing around with a sword—she'd been learning how to make every motion count.

"All right." He paused, eyeing her with concern. "Would you like to go for a swim?"

"That does sound refreshing," she admitted.

He took the sword from her, then set both in the corner of the office—now his room.

"After I change, I'll meet you out there."

She lumbered to her room, closing the door behind her.

"What happened to you?" Sawyer asked. "Did you run through a sprinkler or something?"

Lainie grumbled. "No. Kalen started my sword lessons."

Trying to ignore the cat, she headed into the bathroom, shut the door, and then changed into her suit.

When she came out, the cat made an odd snorting sound. "Ah. Going for a midnight swim. How romantic."

"It's not midnight. And it's not romantic. Get a grip, kitty-cat."

She was tired and not in the mood for his shenanigans. Without another word, she headed to the pool. She set out two towels, then walked straight into the cool water. She sucked in a breath when the waves hit her ribs. The temperature had been fine until then. Embracing the chill against her hot skin, she dove to the bottom, resurfacing near the hot tub.

"Feels good, huh?" Kalen's voice came from the far end of the pool. His rich voice startled her even though she'd known he was also going for a swim.

"Mm, just what I needed." She floated on her back, allowing the water to relax her. It lapped at her arm muscles, shoulders, and neck. She wondered again how sore she'd be tomorrow. She was used to workouts in dance. She also knew what to expect in the aftermath. As she floated, she stared at the clear, star-studded sky. The half-moon shined brightly almost straight overhead.

She heard a splash from Kalen's direction, then felt the water ripple. She sensed him, skimming the bottom, passing beneath her. Another splash indicated he'd surfaced at the other end of the pool. Righting herself, she spun around to find him.

"Thank you for helping me with training," she said. "Part of me still can't see how I'd end up in an actual sword fight, but the rest of me really doesn't want to find out I *should* have trained and didn't."

"You never know what lies ahead," he said. "And it's not just the sword. Learning how to move, how to breathe, how to conserve your strength—that will matter when you're using the timepiece, too. A tired mind makes sloppy magic."

"Isn't that the truth? I'd never suspected magic was real." Or that a hunky man could be conjured from a romance novel. Although, she supposed that fell under the magic heading, too.

Suddenly, in the bushes near the fence, something caught her attention, a glimmer, like moonlight reflecting in someone's eyes. Lainie blinked, wondering if she had imagined the eyes peering out. She shivered. Whatever it was had disappeared. She swam to the ladder, then climbed out. The cold air raised goosebumps over her skin. Hurriedly, she hopped into the hot tub and sank to her chin. Pushing the button to turn on the jets, she relaxed into the pulsating water. *Ah.*

She remained there until her fingers began to prune. "It's time for bed. I'm already drifting off sitting here."

Kalen emerged from the water, then walked over to pick up their towels. After she turned off the jets, she tiredly stood and exited the hot tub. When he handed her a towel, her hand brushed over his. She was aware of him in a way she shouldn't be—as a woman was aware of a man. "Thank you," she said.

"Nae problem."

They each dried before heading inside. Lainie locked the door behind her. "Good night. I'll see you in the morning."

"Good night," he responded.

She went upstairs, noting both kids' lights were off in their rooms. That didn't necessarily mean they were asleep, so she murmured,

"Good night," she said as she passed, receiving quiet responses in return.

As tired as Lainie was, she took a quick shower to wash her hair. If she didn't rinse out the chlorine, she'd be sorry tomorrow. She slipped on her pajamas, dried her hair, and climbed beneath the covers.

As she closed her eyes, she recalled the feeling of Kalen's hand touching hers.

CHAPTER FOUR

It's Never Too Late

"LET ME TAKE A picture," Lainie said to Brennon before he went out the door. Her son looked incredibly handsome. He could melt any girl's heart.

Rolling his eyes, he posed with a blank wall for the backdrop.

"Promise that you'll get some pictures for me of you and Jade."

"I promise, Mom."

She touched his tie, pretending to straighten it because she wanted to feel close to him. He was her baby, and he was growing up too fast.

"Drive safe."

"Always," he said before ducking out the door.

Sighing, she sighed into the kitchen. With Jenna at Sela's, she was completely alone with Kalen. "Would you like to watch some TV?" she asked, motioning toward the living room.

"Yes, that would be fine."

Once there, she turned on the television. Kalen followed her, then sat on the sofa. "I'll be right back. I'm going to make popcorn."

She felt his eyes on her until she turned into the kitchen. She snagged the microwave popcorn from the pantry and prepare it.

Returning, she handed him a bag and took the other end of the sofa. It was easier to watch the television straight on than from one of the side chairs. He shot her a questioning glance.

"Open the top. You can eat it right out of the bag."

He followed her example, tugging the bag open. He was caught off guard by the puff of steam that came out, but once it dissipated, he reached in for his first bite of popcorn. By the third bite, his mouth eased to the side in a lopsided grin, and he nodded. "It's tasty."

"Yep. Did you choose something to watch?"

"No. I was waiting for you. I thought you would make a selection."

"I can." She grabbed the remote from the coffee table, then flipped through a few channels. Finally, she decided on a movie. Her phone jingled, *Karen* flashing on the screen. "Hey, girl, what's up?"

"My schedule is open tomorrow. Would you like to go look for a place in the morning?"

"Sure. That would be great. I think I'd like to look at houses, though, instead of apartments. Is that okay?"

"Yeah. We can do that. I'll print out several listings to check out. It will give us a place to begin."

"Great."

"Nine o'clock? Is it all right if Alaina tags along? It will give us a chance to hang out more."

"Yes, that's fine. See you then." Lainie hung up.

"You are looking for a different house?" Kalen asked.

"Yes. We are only renting this one until the end of the month. That reminds me... I need to see if I can extend our stay here." She made a note on her phone's to-do list. "My friend is a realtor, which means she sells houses. I'm searching for my next, permanent home."

He nodded, seeming to absorb the information. She popped up to grab her computer from the kitchen desk. She'd check again to see what was available on the market. Plus, she should see if she could extend their current lease. Hopefully, she hadn't waited too long to do that.

Lainie strolled back to the sofa, wondering which movie she should select. She gravitated toward fantasy series like Lord of the Rings and Harry Potter. But those wouldn't help Kalen adjust to today's world. She didn't want a romance. Finally, she decided on the original *Top Gun*. It showed a variety of technology and wasn't too violent or lovey-dovey. Plus, she never tired of watching it.

As the previews started up, she tapped on her computer and brought up *Airbnb*. Her account showed the house they currently rented. She checked the availability for the coming month, crossing her fingers and toes, hoping to see green blocks on the calendar. She didn't want to move the kids again. At the moment, she felt like she should have rented it for longer to begin with. At the time, though, she hadn't had the money. Plus, life had been so uncertain. Now, a mere two weeks later and halfway through the rental agreement, everything had changed. The magic money had continued to flow in every day, and her divorce was nearly final. She exhaled a sigh of relief when she found a block of green, showing the house was open until just before Christmas.

After adding another two weeks to their stay, she paid for it. There. Another thing checked off her list. Now, she needed to buckle down to find a permanent house or apartment, but Karen would help with that tomorrow.

Kalen waited patiently at the other end of the sofa for her to start the movie.

She pressed play on the remote. To start with, she explained some of what was on screen, about the men and women who flew fighter jets. "Those are huge machines that fly in the sky, similar to how cars drive on the ground."

"In the air like a bird?"

"They are much bigger than birds. You'll see."

As the opening scene played, Kalen's eyes grew wide with wonder as jets rolled onto the screen, fired up, and took off.

"How?" he asked, stunned by the technology.

Lainie could only give him broad answers. "They have jet engines."

Kalen watched, enthralled by the story, the motorcycles, and the flying scenes. He sat on the edge of his seat, leaning and dodging the action.

"Is this real?" he asked when it was over.

"The jets and things in the movie are real. The story is like a book."

"I'd like to see these jets. Do you know where we can find them?"

Lainie thought for a minute. "I'll check into it. We can see airplanes at the airport. It would be no problem to go by there. But fighter jets like the ones in *Top Gun*, I don't know. I'd have to do some research. Maybe we could go to an air show. There's one in March, but I'm not familiar with any at this time of year."

"I want to see them."

"I'll see what I can do."

"Thank you."

CHAPTER FIVE

Give Me Twelve Hours Sleep

LAINIE OPENED HER EYES, blinking away sleep, struggling to remember where she was. She rolled from her side to her back, staring at the ceiling. She'd been in the middle of a dream she couldn't remember.

Had she truly spent last evening watching television with a dragon shifter?

"Good morning," Sawyer purred.

Reality came tumbling back to her. She groaned. Her alarm blared from the bedstand. She tapped her phone to turn it off. Just a few more minutes. Drawing the covers over her head, she curled up.

The sound of pots and pans rattling in the kitchen drifted to her from downstairs. What on earth? She threw the covers back, sitting with her legs over the side of the bed. A pan crashed against the tile floor. She doubted the kids would be trying to cook. Kalen?

She jumped from the bed, then dashed downstairs. Kalen stood near the stove, trying to shove an extra pan back into its spot in the lower cabinet.

He stood, flashing a grin. "I'm going to make breakfast," he announced.

"You don't need to do that," she said. Where had he gotten that idea?

His gaze dipped to her feet before trailing back up her body. Flushing, she realized she'd worn her shorty pajamas last night. *It isn't a big deal*, she told herself. Everything was covered. More was revealed when she wore her swimsuit.

"I know, but I should contribute around here." After placing two pans on the stove, he opened the refrigerator, taking out eggs, ham, milk, and cheese. He arranged the items on the counter.

Ugh. It was too early to deal with this. In truth, it wasn't that early, but for some reason, she felt groggy. "Coffee," she muttered.

"Of course." He grabbed a pod, then dropped it into the Keurig. The cup was somehow already in place.

"Thank you."

"Nae problem." He set out the coffee creamer and sugar.

She squinted. "How do you know how to do all this?"

"I believe you call it the cooking channel."

"Ah. So that's what you watched when I was gone?"

He began opening more cupboards.

"What are you looking for?"

"Chopping." He made hand motions.

"A cutting board." She pulled one from the cabinet next to the refrigerator, set it on the counter, then sank into a chair.

"Thank you."

He already had a bowl out, into which he proceeded to crack eggs. Then he cut ham, cheese, and onion, before adding them to eggs along, with a little milk. He beat the mixture together, his brow knit in concentration.

"You're making an omelet," she guessed.

"Yes, omelet," he repeated in his Irish accent, which sounded so much better than hers.

The coffee finished brewing, then she doctored her cup. Lifting it, she took a long sip and closed her eyes, waiting for the caffeine to nudge her awake.

Kalen examined the dial on the stove. He didn't seem quite sure how it worked.

"You have to push it in and turn it at the same time. Ten is high heat. One is low. The red light tells you that the stove is on and hot." She rose to demonstrate, then stepped back to allow him to have a go.

He repeated her motions, set the pan on the stove, and poured the egg mixture into the pan.

She found a wooden spoon in the drawer, then handed it to him. "Use this to stir it with."

He nodded.

Lainie set the table, then put bread in the toaster and poured them some OJ.

It was nice of Kalen to fix breakfast, though she would have enjoyed it more if she'd had time to fully wake up first. But evidently, he was wide awake and raring to go.

"Would Brennon and Jenna like some?" he asked.

"I don't think so. Brennon is still in bed. And Jenna is at her friend's house."

"Oh yes. I forgot."

When the eggs were cooked, he spooned them onto the plates. "Thanks," Lainie said, finishing buttering the toast and placing a slice on each plate. "Want to eat at the table or on the porch?"

"You choose," he said.

"I like the porch. I can hear the birds." She set her cup on the Keurig to make a second helping.

They each took their plate and juice out to the porch, then she went back into the kitchen for her coffee. When she returned, she slid the door closed behind her and joined him at the table.

Kalen had waited for her to return before eating.

"It was sweet of you to fix breakfast. Thank you."

"Nae problem. You eat like a bird. You need to eat more."

She laughed at the way he said it with concern in his voice. After taking a bite, she said, "This tastes great."

They ate in silence for several minutes. "When are we going to do our next round of training?" Kalen asked.

She made a face. "I don't think I need more training. After last night, my arms would like twelve hours' sleep and a union rep."

"Felicity charged me with preparing you," he said calmly. "And what you've done so far was only the foundation. You know how to hold a blade now, and how to call the watch. Next, you must learn how to fight without burning yourself out—or calling half the magical world to your doorstep every time you use power."

"We don't go around carrying swords and fighting like in your day," she reminded him. "People call the police when a guy walks down the street with a broadsword, remember?"

His mouth twitched. "Which is why we work on control, not spectacle. Subtle magic. Efficient movement. Saving your strength for when it truly matters."

"I'm going out this morning with my friends," she said. "House hunting. Perhaps we can work on it this afternoon." She still felt like she was stalling, but less than before.

"I'll be ready," he said, as if there had never been any doubt.

With a glance at her phone, she stood, draining the last of her coffee. "I'm going to get dressed. Breakfast was delicious," she told him again. Taking her dishes into the kitchen, she rinsed everything and loaded it all in the dishwasher.

In her bathroom, she closed the door because Sawyer lounged on the windowsill. There was something about the cat that made her wary, something more than his ability to talk. Lainie showered, washed her hair, and blew it dry. She dressed in jeans and a flouncy, floral-print top, then added a dab of blush, mascara, and brow pencil. There—now she was ready for the day.

When she opened the door and came out, Sawyer and Chinchy were nestled on the furry rug near the chairs. "Going out again? Do you ever stay home?" Sawyer muttered.

"When it suits me," she said, not feeling as if she owed the cat an explanation. She moved the magic money from her purse to the duffle. It was becoming a morning habit, one that never got old. She checked the time on her phone. It was almost nine. "Be good while I'm gone. Brennon is home. And Jenna is still at her friend's," she warned.

"Ye of such little faith."

"Yeah. Right."

As Lainie trotted downstairs, she paused outside Brennon's room and said, "I'm going to look at houses. I'll be home around lunchtime."

A groan came in response. Good enough.

Downstairs, she repeated the same to Kalen as he washed the pan he'd cooked with and dried and put it away. The timepiece sat on the counter. She tucked it into her purse.

Her phone chirped with a text from Karen, letting her know they'd pulled up.

Lainie opened the rear door to Karen's Mercedes, slipping onto the luxurious leather seat. "Morning."

"Good morning," Karen said.

"Hi, Lainie," Alaina added. "I hope you don't mind me tagging along. With it being my day off, I just felt like getting out."

"Not at all. It's great to have you with us."

Karen backed out of the driveway. "I have several homes in a variety of price ranges, but only two are in the same school zone. So, how critical is that to you?"

Lainie blew out a breath. "Well, the kids will most likely stay in their schools until the end of this school year. Brennon is graduating, and Jenna will move to high school next year. I'll need to talk to her about a change if we find a house out of this area."

"That could be tough on her," Alaina said.

"Yes. But she knows it's a possibility."

"How about we start with the two homes near here first and then fan out?" Karen asked.

"Sure," Lainie said.

The first was in the Tuscawilla area. Nice homes. Hefty price tags. The house was a spacious four-bedroom with a bonus room over the garage. It had a pool, as so many Florida homes did. But OMG, she hyperventilated over the price tag.

The second was a little farther north, still the same area, but the homes here had more property and were older. This one was three bedrooms, without a bonus room or pool. It was more affordable, but it would require some fixup.

"So from here, I went north to the other side of Altamont, then off I-4. I hope that's all right. There were some promising choices there, which are better priced," Karen explained. "Actually, I live on this side of town."

They looked at four more houses, each one taking them farther from town, all about the same size. Two had pools, but none felt right to Lainie.

"Well, that's it for today," Karen said. "What do you think?"

"I liked the first house the best, but it was the priciest. Probably out of my price range," Lainie said. Yes, she had the magic money, but she didn't know how long that would last. It could stop tomorrow.

"We can look again next weekend if you're up to it after Thanksgiving," Karen said. "I have a B list. Not that they're inferior, just in a different area."

Lainie wasn't sure she liked this area so far from the kids' schools. For Brennon, it just meant a longer commute until he graduated. And Jenna would be changing schools anyway, but this would mean she wouldn't go to the same high school as her friends. She dipped her head, studying her hands. In the front seats, Karen and Aliana discussed the Lake Brantley area, which was where Alaina lived, and how one resident flew a seaplane in on occasion to bring in guests.

Lainie's gaze caught on her purse and the purplish glow emanating from within it. She peeked inside. Why was it glowing? Cautiously, she looked up, but no one had noticed. It wasn't like she could take it out and examine it now. How would she explain the glow to Karen and Alaina?

She stared out the window, willing the timepiece to chill. The area they were in now was rural countryside. Maybe Karen had taken a different route home. Lainie didn't recall passing this way earlier. A *FOR SALE* sign caught her eye. It was for a property with a large house set back off the road.

Lainie leaned forward, resting her hand on the seatback in front of her. "Stop. Go back. I want to see this place. It's for sale."

"Really? It seems like quite a lot of property. I thought you wanted a subdivision," Karen said.

"Well, that's what I thought." Was it her imagination, or was the glow coming from her purse now stronger? "But something about this place intrigues me."

Karen pulled into a driveway to turn around. She drove to the entrance of the property. A sign read: *Vineyard Homestead For Sale, twenty-two acres, owner-financing available*.

Lainie's heart sped up. The glow intensified. She moved her purse to the floor.

"That's a lot of land. You still want to take a look?" Karen asked.

"Oh yes."

Karen drove through the stone-enhanced entrance and up a long, private road until they came to a Y. To the right sat a two-story house with a circular drive. To the left, there were a couple of large buildings. They turned toward the house and parked in the driveway.

Lainie stepped from the car. As soon as her feet hit the ground, she felt a deep vibration inside her. It felt like she belonged there, which was totally insane. She had no intention of purchasing a winery.

Lainie grabbed her purse to take with her. Given the way Sarah had tried to get her hands on the timepiece, Lainie had no idea if someone might try to steal it.

Karen got out, peering at her over the car's roof. "Well?"

"I want to see it. Get more information."

"Let's go then," Karen said, walking toward the door. Alaina joined them.

Karen knocked. A slender, older man with graying hair opened the door. He had kind eyes, which crinkled around the edges. "May I help you?"

"We were out house hunting and saw your sign," Karen said.

"Something about the place intrigues me. Can you tell us about it?" Lainie chimed in, unable to help herself.

"Sure. Come in." The man smiled. "I'm Charles Lambert, but everyone calls me Charlie. My wife and I built the house in 1996. We started the vines in 2000. Sue passed away earlier this year. The vineyard was mainly her baby. We never had children, so I'm ready to sell it. Maybe move to Georgia to be closer to my family. I have a brother and sister in Athens."

"It's a beautiful house," Lainie said, admiring the high ceilings, the staircase set on the right, and the walking bridge that cut across overhead, which divided the entrance from the living room.

"The house is 3500 square feet, four bedrooms, plus an office and game room. I have a pool table in there that can stay with the house." He walked into the living room, and they followed.

The kitchen was to the right of the living room. It had a large commercial stove and range. Sue must have liked to cook or entertain, Lainie guessed. There was an island with a sink, similar to her rental but much larger. In the corner, there was a door that probably led to a walk-in pantry.

To the left of the kitchen, situated like an L, was a family room with a fireplace and a large flatscreen mounted on the wall. French doors in both the living room and family room led to a deck and swimming pool with a hot tub.

"There are two master suites. One is on the ground floor. The other is upstairs. It is separated from another three bedrooms by the bridge and a large seating area." Charlie led the way, showing them the downstairs master bedroom, huge bathroom, and closet area. Then they went upstairs to view those bedrooms.

The layout would allow Kalen to take the room downstairs. That way, he could have his privacy, and the kids could have theirs.

"The house is beautiful," Lainie said.

"Thank you. Sue and I enjoyed many happy years here."

"What about the winery? Are you selling the house separately?" Karen asked.

"Together," he said. "I'll be happy to show it to you if you'd like."

"Yes," Lainie said a little too enthusiastically—forget fancy negotiating. Karen glared at her. Lainie shrugged a shoulder.

"Let's go through the garage. I have a golf cart there." After Charlie opened the garage door, they all hopped on, Lainie in the front, and Alaina and Karen in the back. He drove them around the side of the small lake.

"There are three buildings on this side. The winery with its wine cellar, a barn, and a cottage, which is the original house that came with the property. We used it as a guesthouse, but also rented it out for a while."

Lainie's entire body thrummed with anticipation as she walked through the winery. She couldn't explain it; but she had a soul-deep desire to possess this property.

"What's the asking price?" Lainie blurted out. She stood in the doorway, looking to the left at the rows of vines. She was already in love with the place. Whether she could afford it or not, was another matter.

Charlie studied her. "One point five million."

Her knees went weak. She drew herself taller to keep them from buckling. Well, no winery for her.

"I'm offering to finance for the right buyer," he said.

With a spark in her eye, Alaina said, "Perhaps we should talk about a partnership."

Karen joined in, "Are you thinking about group ownership? Like maybe an investment by the bougie babes?"

Lainie glanced from one friend to the other. Karen shrugged. "That's a possibility. I purchase investment properties from time to time. We can discuss it."

"I can't let you do that," Lainie whispered. "I'll find something else. It's just a house." But she knew she wouldn't. Not like this. Not like it was part of her beating heart. Her mind spun with all the possibilities the winery had.

She could make it a wedding venue. Maybe rent out the cottage, hire people to run the winery, or keep the staff Charlie had.

"How long has it been on the market?" Karen asked.

"I only put the sign in the yard yesterday. You're the first to look at it."

Karen nodded. "Can you give us a week to decide?"

"Of course. I'm not in any hurry."

"Good," Alaina said.

Lainie wasn't convinced. She was used to living in a trailer and saving her pennies. Sure, she had some money now. The magic money had grown to eight hundred and fifty thousand dollars. But that didn't seem real. And she couldn't spend it without John knowing something was up.

"You have a beautiful place," Lainie told Charlie. "We'll be in touch."

"You know where to find me."

He drove them back to their car. They changed vehicles and Karen drove away. As they turned onto the highway, Lainie noticed that the glow from her purse had stopped. What did that mean?

"I'm going to do a little research about the property," Karen said. "But that is an incredible buy. The vineyard and winery alone are probably worth that much."

"Well, you know I'm in. Should we ask the other gals?" Alaina said.

"Wait a minute. We're talking about the place I'm going to live. My home," Lainie said. "I don't think I want a group investment for that."

"I'm sure we can work something out," Karen said.

"Maybe we can divide it up. I purchase the house, and we buy the vineyard and winery operation as partners. That could be a possibility." The reality was if the magic money stopped, that would be the best she could do. But if it kept coming...she might be able to swing the entire purchase.

"Do we need a lawyer to make sure everything is kosher," Alaina added.

"I have a lawyer in mind," Lainie said.

"Since my business is a brokerage, I can handle the deal," Karen said.

"So, what do you think? Should we call a girls' meeting and include them, or just go with the three of us?" Alaina asked.

"Let's handle it between us for now," Karen said. "If that's okay with you gals. I'll do a workup on it. Then we'll know what's what."

"Then I'll decide what direction I want to go," Lainie said. It would be her place. She should make the decision.

"Sounds good," Alaina said.

Karen turned into Lainie's subdivision. Two police cars were at the end of her street with their lights flashing. Lainie's heart felt like rocks in her throat. What was going on? Had John finally lost it over the divorce? Were the kids, okay?

CHAPTER SIX

Don't Test Me

KAREN STOPPED HER CAR next to the police vehicle. The car had barely stopped when Lainie flew out and ran across the lawn. She rushed alongside the police car where one officer stood.

"What's going on?" she asked the officer, tamping down her sense of panic.

"There's a guy with a screw loose, walking around brandishing a sword."

Lainie's heart beat wildly in her chest.

"What?" Her gaze shifted to the yard two houses down to where the other officer stood, his hands on his hips, with his thick shoulders rolled forward. Even from where she stood, with his back to her, she couldn't help but notice his red hair. When she looked just beyond him... OMG. The guy with the screw loose was Kalen. Bare-chested, he stood in his swim trunks like a magnificent gladiator, a broadsword in his hand.

She fetched the timepiece from her purse. If it could have power over something, she needed it now.

Lainie glanced to the side, noting the neighbor with her nose pressed to the window and a scowl on her face. There were benefits to not living in a neighborhood where everyone knew each other's business. No doubt, she was the person who contacted the police.

"Just place the sword on the ground," she heard the officer say.

"Oh no," she whispered. To the officer beside her, she said, "That's my friend. He's staying at my house. He's harmless, but he sleepwalks and gets caught up in his dreams. Can you take me over to him?"

She lucked out, when the agreeable officer obliged her. The young, blond-haired officer had kind brown eyes. He seemed to understand her plight and escorted her to where his partner and Kalen were. "Kalen, what are you doing out here? You need to wake up and go inside."

"They were trying to get into the house."

"Who was?" she asked.

"Goblins. They were looking for the magic."

"What's he talking about?" Officer Blondie asked.

"He seems to dream in fantasy—like *Harry Potter* sorts of things. He has the soul of a protector." Lainie explained.

She blew out a frustrated huff of air. "Well, they're gone now. Put the sword on the ground and let's go back into the house. When you wake up, we can talk about it." She wasn't sure if he would do as she asked. She didn't want to mention that the officers might take him away if he didn't. Lord, she hoped it didn't come to that.

"The goblins are gone?" he stated, setting the sword on the ground.

Lainie drew on movies for her explanation to the officer. "I'll just take him back inside, put him in bed, and let him sleep this off. He'll eventually wake up from the dream."

"Are you sure, ma'am?" Officer Blondie asked.

"Absolutely." Lainie inched closer to Kalen, then picked up the sword. Jeez, it was heavy. She began walking with him, guiding him toward the front door, with the timepiece in her hand at his back.

"What's with the sword?" Officer Red asked.

"We're trying out fencing. We use different types of swords—rapier, épée, saber," she rattled off. Jenna participated in the fencing club at school. Of course, this sword was one she'd listed, but it was the only explanation that popped into her head. She hoped the officers didn't know the difference. They didn't comment, so she felt a hint of relief.

"I'll put him to bed," she said.

"Are you sure he's okay?" Blondie asked.

"Yes. He doesn't usually dream about battling goblins." Lainie wasn't even sure what a goblin was. She glanced past the officers to Karen and Alaina. The women seemed frozen, their mouths hanging open.

By the time Lainie directed Kalen through the front door, the officers had returned to their respective vehicles, ready to leave. She directed Kalen to the sofa, setting the sword on the coffee table. She still clutched the timepiece in her other hand. "Stay put. We'll talk about this in a moment."

Lanie went to the large picture window, peering at the street. The police cars turned their lights off before driving away. Karen pulled into the driveway. She and Alaina got out, then marched up the sidewalk.

Oh boy.

Lainie opened the door just as Karen began to knock. "Sorry about that. I have a house guest staying with us. He's the brother of a friend." She kept with the same story she'd told the kids.

"Are you okay?" Alaina asked as she attempted to peek inside.

"Yeah. Sure. Come on in," Lainie told them. She didn't want to be rude and shut the door in their faces, but she didn't care to have them near Kalen, either. Still, she stepped back to allow them entrance.

"Gals, this is Kalen. He's visiting from Ireland, staying with me for a while. Kalen, these are my friends, Karen and Alaina."

He rose from the sofa, giving them a nod. "Pleased to meet you."

Lainie thought she heard a throaty purr escape Alaina. "Likewise."

"Nice to meet you," Karen said.

Lainie glanced toward the stairs as Brennon trotted into the kitchen. His hair was disheveled. Obviously, he'd just rolled out of bed. "Good morning."

He'd gotten in late last night after the Homecoming dance. So, he'd slept in longer than usual, seemingly unaware of the fiasco that had taken place outside. Jenna hadn't returned yet from spending the night with her friend. Fortunately, both kids had been spared from seeing this episode.

But what about the next one? an insidious voice whispered inside her head. She pushed it aside.

"Good morning, honey. These are my friends, Alaina and Karen. Gals, my son Brennon. He went to a Homecoming dance last night and didn't get home until the wee hours of the morning, hence the reason he's just getting up after noon."

Brennon waved. "Hi."

"Nice to meet you," Karen said.

"Did you have fun at the dance?" Alaina asked.

Brennon smiled, his face turning pink. "Yes. It was great." He headed into the kitchen. She watched as he got the OJ from the fridge, poured a glass, and downed it.

Lainie turned her attention back to her friends, who eyed Kalen. She didn't want to encourage a conversation about him. Wouldn't they suspect there was something amiss with a guy who wielded a sword in his swim trunks and chased after goblins? "So, perhaps we should get together next weekend to discuss the business idea. It will give Karen time to research the property. Let us all mull over whether we want to do this or not."

"What is your rental situation here?" Karen asked.

"I extended our stay until mid-December."

"That's good. It will give us more time. With owner-financing, though, there's an opportunity to move things along more quickly than if we were dealing with a bank."

"That's great," Lainie said. She hesitated. The buying-a-home deal opened a can of worms in terms of money. She couldn't work through a bank because she'd have to move her funds through them. That wouldn't work. Technically, no one knew about her magic money. Maybe she should just rent a home.

The front door opened. Jenna danced through, juggling her overnight bag, giving the door a nudge with her foot to close it. She glanced around. "Oh, hi," she giggled, seeming self-conscious that everyone's attention was focused on her.

"Jenna, I'd like you to meet two of my friends from college. Alaina and Karen, this is Jenna, my daughter.."

"Hi," Jenna said again.

"Hello," Karen said.

Alaina waved. "Hi there."

"How was Sela's?" Lainie asked.

"Awesome. We had fun." Jenna scooted into the kitchen to join Brennon, dropping her bag near the stairs. Bitsy dashed over to greet her, begging for attention. Jenna lifted the pup, tucking her in the crook of her arm. She grabbed a drink, then she and Brennon headed upstairs, chatting as they went.

Lainie turned back to her friends. Kalen rose. "Excuse me." He strolled past them, completely oblivious to the women's appreciative stares, and went into his room.

Alaina fanned her face with her hand. "I think I want to live at your house."

"If nothing else, we should have our next girls' night out here. Fabulous entertainment." Karen moved toward the front door.

"He's only visiting," Lainie said.

"All the better," Alaina replied.

"You're divorced. You want to go through that again?" Lainie asked, making a face.

"Who's talking about marriage? But it's fun to window shop," Alaina said.

Lainie walked them to the door. "I'll get in touch about the time for Friday. And if you find anything out about the property in the meantime, you can text me."

"Okay. Sounds good," Karen said.

"Have a nice Thanksgiving," Lainie said with a smile.

"You too," Alaina called back.

Lainie closed the door, leaning her back against it for several minutes. Jeez, that was awkward. She marched to Kalen's room and knocked. "Kalen, can we talk?"

He opened the door. "Of course."

She turned and walked to the kitchen to prepare a cup of coffee. He tagged along. "Would you like a cup?" she asked.

"Yes, please."

She fixed them each a cup, handing him one. "Let's sit on the porch." It was further away from the kids.

Though the idea of laying into him for wielding a sword outside was tempting, she controlled herself, sipping her coffee. "Okay. Tell me what happened that made you take a sword outside."

"I was swimming in the pool when four goblins materialized among the shrubs. They're ugly little buggers, extremely fast, and can shapeshift into animals or humans. Two were carrying swords. They must have sensed the magic in the house, maybe the box since the timepiece was with you. The goblins tried to sneak over to the patio. When I shouted, they broke some of the flowerpots, throwing them at me." He paused for a moment, giving a nod to the broken pots scattered about. "I dashed into the house to get my sword. But by the time I came outside again, they were rounding the corner and heading through the gate out to the front yard. I followed them, ready to dispatch them back to the spirit realm. But I never got a chance. They were already at the front door, and when they discovered it was locked, they turned and fled."

Lainie swallowed. This was getting serious. "Do you really think they'll come back?"

"Probably. They don't give up easily. Once they set their sights on something, they egg each other on. And gaining a magic bauble is right up their alley. They're like hyenas—they go after easy targets. They run in packs and are very socialized creatures. They love to cause trouble."

"Hyenas?" Lainie shivered.

"Goblins don't eat people." He laughed. "But they have few scruples about killing someone who stands in the way of what they want."

She was instantly worried about Brennon and Jenna's safety—and unexpectedly grateful Kalen had put a sword in her hand yesterday. She'd never truly believed she might need it. The lesson had left her sore and exhausted, but now she understood: it hadn't just been about learning how to swing. It had been about learning how quickly her strength could drain in a real fight, how fast her body could hit its limits.

And in the here-and-now, people didn't use swords in the middle of subdivisions. She needed options that wouldn't get her arrested—or leave her too spent to protect her kids. She drew in a slow breath, then let it out deliberately. Her nerves crackled, sending warning signals into her mind and heart. If calamity or evil ever touched her family, she'd never forgive herself. No amount of magic money, no vineyard, no fresh start was worth even a scratch on her children.

Her muscles tightened around her heart. "Maybe I should box the timepiece up and tuck it away again."

"I think that's impossible. It's too late for that. The magic has claimed you. It's been entrusted to you."

"For what purpose?"

"Only you can determine that. But it will take time," Kalen said.

Lainie was confused. She would have to take the bad with the good. No, she refused that idea. There must be a way to *stop* the bad, and prevent anything disastrous from happening.

Then she remembered that knowledge was power—and in her case, survival. She needed to learn everything she could about the timepiece and the creatures it attracted, and she needed Felicity's and Kalen's training to do more than make her feel brave. It had to make her ready.

CHAPTER SEVEN

My Balance Is Off

TODAY SHE WAS A millionaire.

Lainie did the math as she awoke with a groan and peeled her sore body from the bed. It was day twenty. Twenty days ago, outside the pawn shop where she'd actually been considering selling her grandmother's pocket watch, the timepiece had started giving her money. Those daily gifts now added up to one million dollars.

She sat, then stood, her arm and shoulder muscles protesting fiercely with only the smallest movement. She padded over to her purse to make sure today's magic money had arrived.

She dumped the contents of her purse onto the bed. Yes, yes, *YES.* She gave an arm-pump into the air and suffered the pangs of stressed muscles. She didn't care.

The thought tickled her insides. She couldn't stop smiling. Moaning at her sore muscles, she put the money away in the closet, but a few aches and pains couldn't spoil her joy. The duffle bag wouldn't even close. The stacks of money overflowed onto the floor. It was ridiculous in a good way.

As great as it was, it wasn't enough to buy the vineyard property outright. But it may be enough to negotiate a financial arrangement with the owner, perhaps even without her friends joining in.

She stripped off the nightshirt. *OMG.* Every muscle in her torso screamed. She padded into the bathroom. Even though she'd showered and washed her hair last night before going to bed, she clipped up her hair and stepped beneath a hot, forceful spray of water, hoping it would relieve her muscles. She wanted her body to feel as delightful as her spirits.

By the time she towel-dried, her muscles had loosened, and she felt less sore. She knew tomorrow would be worse. Muscles always protested more the second day after any new kind of physical workout.

She dressed, selecting an outfit with pockets. That way, the time-piece could always be close. Then she called her mom to let her know they would be bringing a guest with them to Thanksgiving dinner and to confirm what she would bring to contribute to the feast. Each family brought something, usually their same "specialty" year after year. Her mom and dad were in charge of the turkey, dressing, and gravy. Matt and his wife, Glenda, fixed the mashed potatoes. Robbie and Lexi brought green-bean casserole. Tony and Mandie did sweet-potato casserole. Crystal baked pies. And Lainie baked bread and usually made a fruit salad.

That was their Thanksgiving routine. Sometimes, one of her brothers would have to travel to his wife's family, and on those years, their dish contribution would have to be picked up by one of the other siblings. But this year, they'd all be there, along with the eleven grandchildren.

When her aunts and uncles were alive, they'd sometimes join them. It was how her mom did Thanksgiving. It was how her mom came by her more-the-merrier philosophy. Lainie's grandparents on her mom's side had been the same way. And they occasionally included friends, the pastor, or someone who would otherwise be spending the holiday alone. It was a way of life that John had never experienced since he was an only child. Her family gatherings were loud and rowdy with a lot of laughter.

And she wouldn't change a minute of it.

After the call, Lainie's morning progressed the way it did most days, only she couldn't stop smiling. All the way to and from taking Jenna to school. Since it was Monday, she'd teach dance classes this evening. She wrote a note for Brennon to fix spaghetti for dinner, arranging the ingredients in plain sight. She and Jenna would eat after classes.

Back home, with both kids at school, Lainie made a second cup of coffee and sat outside on the porch. This had become her favorite place in the rental. She enjoyed looking over the pool and taking in the fresh air. And for the first time since arriving home yesterday to the police out front, she was able to think about the winery and house she'd seen yesterday.

It was bizarre, but she itched to buy it. Before she'd set foot on the property, a place like that wasn't even on her radar. But now, she could close her eyes and picture so many opportunities. She could hire people to grow the grapes and run the winery, turn it into a wedding venue, and maybe even have a little shop. It would be the business that could support them when the magical money stopped. *All good things must come to an end*, as the saying went. She imagined the money would, too.

She hoped it would hold out a little longer, though.

Kalen cracked open the slider. "May I join you?"

"Sure." She hadn't seen him this morning. He must have been lingering in his room. He looked fresh and clean-shaven, with his chin-length hair falling perfectly into place.

When he came out, taking a seat in the other lounge chair, Bitsy snuck out as well. The pup ran to her favorite spot in the back corner of the yard and sniffed around.

"How are you feeling this morning?" he asked.

She moaned. "Like I've been hit by a truck. Every muscle from my waist up aches."

"I'm sorry to hear that." He gazed at her over the rim of his coffee mug.

For the zillionth time, she was struck by his handsome face and mischievous grin. The man was way too fit and good-looking for an aging gal like her. Not that she put the two of them together exactly.

"This week's schedule will be different. The kids have Wednesday off from school due to Thanksgiving. I know it's not something you've celebrated, so if you'd like, I can set the computer up, and you can read about it."

"Yes. I'd be interested in trying that."

"Okay. I'll set it up. I left instructions for Brennon to prepare dinner."

"I'll be glad to help."

"Thank you. My son needs his turn in the kitchen so that he can learn to cook. Spaghetti is his specialty dish." She chuckled.

"I'll be glad to help any time you need it."

"I know. Thanks." Bitsy trotted over, wanting into her lap. She lifted the pup and stood, then picked up her empty coffee mug and headed inside. "I'll get the computer up and running."

Letting the dog hop from her arms, she moved the computer from the kitchen desk to the breakfast counter, first having to slide the swords out of the way. Kalen must have set them there in anticipation of more training. Not. They needed to choose a place to store them.

Opening the computer, she fired it up and logged in. After putting the name of the property in the search field, the listing for the winery filled the screen. The picture didn't do it justice. The information gave her more insight into the wine-making operation, though. There were nineteen-thousand vines on the property, and they produced a variety of wines. Although the owner wanted to sell it all as one, to Lainie, it was two separate opportunities. One for a home. The other for a business. If she had a little more money, she could buy both outright. Wouldn't that be fabulous? But owning the winery with her friends would be great, also.

Now everything needed to fall into place.

Kalen strolled up beside her.

"Have a seat," she told him. Moving the laptop closer to him so he could see. "A computer is similar to the TV and phone. Information flows through it and you view it on the screen. This area is called the mouse pad. It controls the cursor or arrow location on the screen."

"Why is it called a mouse? It looks nothing like a mouse."

She shrugged. "Let's not get into that."

"Anyway, you just slide your finger around this square, and as your finger moves, the cursor moves around on the screen. See? And once it's on top of the item you want to select, you click this lower corner." Kalen looked fascinated but puzzled. Then she pointed out the Google icon. "When you select this, it takes you to the internet, which is like a library full of information." The search box opened on the screen. "Then you type in the subject you're interested in." She typed in chocolate cake. "Then press the enter key, and it will give you a list to choose from, click on one, and voila, read what it has to say."

Kalen nodded, seeming to get a general idea.

"Here's one called Hersheyland. Hmm, I'm not familiar with that company. I move the cursor and tap it. And it takes us to their website. There's a recipe for Perfectly Chocolate Chocolate Cake." She made a mental note to visit the site again.

"Now you try. Type in Thanksgiving." She stood and moved behind him, so that she could see over his shoulder. Her nose filled with his spicy scent.

He started typing, using his index finger, pecking out one letter at a time. He paused and sat back in the chair. "Now hit enter," she said, showing him the key.

He did. A list showed. "Now using one finger on the mousepad, slide it until you have the cursor over which site you want to go to." With his heavy-handed touch, the cursor started zipping all over the screen. "Use a gentle touch. It doesn't take much to move it." She placed her hand atop his, guiding him while enjoying the connection a bit too much.

"There you go," she said, having clicked on the Wikipedia link. "Now you can read about Thanksgiving. Just play around and see what you find." She patted his shoulder and left him to experiment.

"Okay. Thank you."

Lainie had a small list of things to do today. Water the potted plants, wash the linens, and create her Thanksgiving shopping list. She thought she had everything she needed for baking the bread, but she checked the pantry to be sure. Flour and yeast were the main ingredients. Yep. She would buy the fruit on Wednesday to make sure it was fresh.

Next, she stripped the beds and tossed the sheets in the washing machine. While that was going, she watered the potted plants on the front porch. There was a watering can in the garage, so she used that, filling it in the kitchen sink. She wondered what the owners would do if the renters didn't take care of them. She would think the yard service would tend to them, but she noticed they were looking droopy. There was a tall pot holding a mixture of plants including caladiums, and two hanging baskets of impatiens. She gave them each a cool drink.

Then she refilled the can to do the ones in the back, remembering she still had to clean up the mess of broken pots, thanks to the apparent goblin attack the day before. The plants around the pool deck had survived their rampage, and since they got rain, they seemed to be in good shape. She watered the six that remained on the covered porch. The Chinese evergreen had several brown leaves at the bottom. She plucked them from the plant. As she stepped back, something touched her shoulder.

She twisted her head, screaming at the sight of a thin, ugly creature with pointed ears standing inches behind her. Her shock was so great, the watering can fell from her hand and crashed on the deck. There were three other creatures standing about four feet away, as if waiting their turn to harass her.

"The watch if you please," the goblin said.

She recoiled, trying to step around him. "It's mine. It won't work for anyone else."

"It's magic. And magic can be coaxed," another goblin said.

The sliding door slid open until it banged against the other end of the track. Kalen framed the doorway, sword in hand. Lainie used the moment of surprise to duck and scoot past him into the house. The goblin beside her accomplished the same move, fast as lightning, seeming glued to her side.

Once in the living room, the goblin's long fingers latched onto her wrist. He flashed his teeth in a wicked grin as he pulled out a short blade.

"If you kill me, you'll never get the talisman."

"Who said anything about killing you?" Stumpy laughed. He seemed to be the smallest of the bunch. She reminded herself that powerful things could come in small packages.

If he didn't want her dead, then why the knife? It dawned on her that pain was a means to encourage people to spill what they know. Fear shot through her.

She fired a glance toward where Kalen had been. He had gone after the other three goblins. If she were going to get away, it would be up to her. Mustering every ounce of strength in her, she thrust her arm downward, at the same time kicking her leg up and planting her foot squarely on his chest—just like the front-kick drills she'd done in long-ago fitness classes, except this time the target wasn't a padded bag.

Shocked, the goblin loosened his grip enough for her to break free. She sprinted into the kitchen and swept the sword from the counter, fingers locking tight around the hilt. The familiar weight dragged at her tired muscles, but her body remembered what Kalen had drilled into her: **small, clean movements; let your legs do the work; save your strength.**

She turned. The goblin closed in, eyes wild as he raised his knife. Lainie didn't think—there wasn't time for thinking. Training and pure self-preservation took over. She brought the broadsword up and then down in a tight diagonal, not a wild swing, driving the motion from her legs and hips the way Kalen had insisted. The blade cut through the air in an efficient arc.

The goblin's eyes rounded. His fingers spasmed; the knife slipped from his grip and hit the tile with a clank.

Then, with a fiery spark and a sharp crack, he vanished. Gone.

Lainie spun to see Kalen slice the head off the last goblin outside. The same spark and crack sounded again.

Lainie dropped her sword to the floor. She ran around to the kitchen sink, where she leaned over, sure she was going to lose her breakfast. Her stomach calmed as she took several deep breaths. Then she splashed water on her face.

"I can't believe that just happened," she said as the ill feeling passed. Her arms still trembled faintly, and her legs felt like overcooked spaghetti.

"You did well," Kalen said as he stepped inside and closed the sliding door. He was breathing a little harder, but nowhere near as spent as she felt. His gaze flicked to the sword at her feet, then back to her face. "You remembered your footing. You kept the strike tight. You didn't freeze."

"I also almost threw up on the kitchen floor," she muttered. "Pretty sure that wasn't covered in training."

One corner of his mouth lifted. "You're not meant to feel nothing after your first real fight. But you stayed on your feet. That matters. We'll work on keeping your balance and saving more of your strength next time."

"What happened to them? Where did they go?"

Sawyer stood on the dining table and stretched. "They're from another dimension. When you killed them, they returned there."

Lainie nodded, although she couldn't grasp the idea of another dimension. "I don't want anything to do with that."

"Like it or not," Kalen said quietly, "I think you're already connected to it. All the more reason to keep training—smarter, not just harder."

Later that afternoon, as Lainie picked up Jenna from school and drove to the dance studio, she couldn't shake the feeling of being watched. She never saw anything, but she kept looking over her shoulder. She couldn't tell whether she was being paranoid or if something was really out there, lingering, waiting to pounce.

Since she was in a moving vehicle, she decided on paranoid. Jenna hopped in the van, so Lainie pushed her concerns aside. "How was your day?"

"Okay. I have a ton of homework due tomorrow though. It seems every teacher decided we needed an assignment before the holiday break."

"I'm sorry. Hopefully, you can get a lot done during the hour between your dance classes."

"Yeah. I'm going to try."

"That's my girl."

Out of the corner of her eye, Lainie saw Jenna make a face. She had to remember that her budding teenager didn't appreciate that sort of comment.

Lainie parked in the studio parking lot, got out of the van, and grabbed her dance bag from the rear. She scanned the lot, eyeing the other cars.

"Don't worry. I don't see Dad's truck," Jenna said.

Her daughter referred to the incident two weeks ago, when John had made a scene here. "No. I think your dad has moved past the 'trying-to-change-my-mind' stage and into acceptance. At least I hope so." Then she muttered under her breath, "Of course, he can be manic."

Like always, as soon as she stepped into the studio and began teaching the children, everything about the outside world and her troubles faded.

CHAPTER EIGHT

I Need a Makeover

THE DELICIOUS AROMA OF spaghetti and garlic bread greeted them as they walked in the house after dance class. The table was set, and Kalen handed her a glass of wine as soon as she walked into the kitchen.

"How was dance?" Brennon asked.

"Great." Lainie sipped her wine, then tipped her head back with a sigh. It felt good to be home and to see that everyone was okay. As soon as class had ended, the thread of tension running through her returned.

"Have a seat. We're ready to eat," Brennon said.

Kalen sliced the garlic bread. It looked as though he and Brennon had been working together to prepare dinner. The act of kindness on Kalen's part warmed her heart.

It was nine-thirty by the time they gathered around the table. "You guys could have gone ahead and eaten without us. But thanks for waiting."

"We snacked," Brennon said with a smile.

Everyone was so hungry that they devoured their food without conversation. As Lainie took her empty plate to the kitchen, she said to Brennon, "Jenna had a lot of homework dumped on her for tonight. What about you?"

"Naw. I only had one subject, and it's done."

"Lucky," Jenna pouted.

"Well, you can finish it up. I'll do the dishes. I'm beat. I'll be turning in early," Lainie said. "Did you feed the critters?"

"Yes. They're all taken care of. Bitsy turned her nose up at the food, but she finally ate."

"Thanks. And thanks for fixing dinner, Brennon," she said.

"Kalen helped."

"Thank you also, Kalen."

"Nae problem." His gaze held hers a bit longer than usual. She liked his version of "you're welcome."

Lainie recalled the linens she'd washed earlier, telling the kids, "Your sheets are washed. Please make your beds."

"Okay. Thanks."

They drifted away from the table, clearing it as they went, before disappearing upstairs. Lainie rinsed the plates, then loaded the dishwasher. She made quick work of the pans. Kalen dried them and stacked them near the stove. "Thank you," Lainie said when they were finished.

"Anytime." Kalen hesitated. "Are you okay after the incident earlier today?"

"Yes. I was shaken up at first, but I'm better now."

He nodded.

"I'm tired, though. I'm going to bed. You can stay up and watch TV if you'd like."

"No. I'm turning in also. Good night."

Lainie lay in bed staring at the ceiling. She was bone tired, yet every time she closed her eyes, she saw the pointy face and thin cheekbones of a goblin. A little over a week ago, she'd had a dragon sleeping in her room. She'd thought that was a bundle of trouble. She'd had no idea what trouble could amount to. A shiver ran through her at the memory of fighting the goblin and sending him back to where he'd come from. She had no idea if that meant he was dead or alive. Dead, she assumed given that she'd stabbed him with a sword.

Now she worried about what other creatures would be after the timepiece.

Sometime between worry and counting blessings she fell asleep. Lainie woke on Tuesday still incredibly sore from her Saturday training session. But it had been worth the pain to know she'd helped send the goblins home again, wherever that was—and that the hours Kalen had spent harping on stance, balance, and economy hadn't just been theory.

Today seemed like it lacked purpose. She decided to concentrate on the timepiece, treating it like homework for a class she'd never signed up for but couldn't drop. She spent hours on the computer trying to decipher the insignias etched along the sides.

By mid-afternoon, she had several pages of notes and drawings. No clear answers yet, but this was a different kind of training than swinging a sword—slow, patient, brain-tiring instead of muscle-tiring. And if knowledge really was power, she needed every scrap she could get.

Wednesday was Thanksgiving prep day. The kids were home from school and slept in. Lainie hummed as she prepared the bread mixture, then set it aside in a large mixing bowl to rise. After feeding the animals, she had time to run to the grocery store to pick up the berries for the fruit salad while the dough did its thing.

Kalen strolled from his bedroom and fixed his coffee. He looked scorching hot, wearing a black-and-gray graphic tee shirt with a knight kneeling with the tip of his sword buried in the ground. She hadn't paid much attention to what he'd selected when last they'd shopped. But, oh man, did it hug his muscular frame. As did the black denim pants.

She swallowed hard.

He smiled, completely unaware of how gorgeous he looked. "Good morning." He leaned against the kitchen counter to drink his coffee.

"I'm going to Publix. Want to ride along with me?" she asked. She figured it would allow him an opportunity to deal with the real world before meeting her parents on Thursday. She was a little nervous about that. What would they think of him? What would her brothers think?

"Sure," Kalen answered.

"Okay. We'll leave in five minutes."

Lainie hurried upstairs and got her purse, then waited for him at the door to the garage. He was right behind her. When she pushed open the door, he reached above her to hold it open while she went out to the van.

"Thanks," she said at his attempt to help.

In the grocery store, he took the grocery basket from her as soon as she picked it up.

"I'll carry it," he said.

It was a gentlemanly offer, something she wasn't used to. She led the way to the produce section, then filled the basket with in-season fruit, then added a bag of coconut, tiny colored marshmallows, and a container of frozen Cool Whip. She preferred fresh fruit, but it could be made with canned in a pinch.

"Would you like anything while we're here?" she asked Kalen.

"They have so much. It's not like our simple markets."

"I imagine it's quite different."

"Do they have dried jerky?"

"Beef jerky? Yes." She led him to the section of jerky and summer sausages.

"Mmm. Yes." He purred in a deep, rumbling voice.

She put a couple of packages of jerky in the basket as well as some sausage. "Brennon may enjoy this also."

Every aisle they went down people turned and stared at Kalen. He was a large man with a muscular physique. And he moved with a sense of power and authority. Definitely noticeable.

They'd run out of room in the basket—she tended to do that and usually wished she'd chosen a cart. On the way to the cash register, she picked up two bottles of wine, one white and one red.

Lainie set the wine on the conveyer belt, and Kalen unloaded the basket. The cashier's gaze roamed over Kalen, her mouth pulling into an appreciative smile. Lainie wondered if the woman even noticed her standing a short distance away. "I need your ID," the cashier said to him.

He lifted a brow at Lainie. "I'm getting the food," she said to the woman as she slipped her ID from her wallet.

The cashier took it, glancing between Lainie and Kalen. She chuckled and gave the slightest shake of her head, as if the two of them didn't go together. For a second, Lainie wondered if that was what the woman was thinking, then she decided she didn't care.

The little voice of "not good enough" reared its ugly head.

She tamped it down as she paid for their items. Kalen gathered two of the three bags. She took the third, and they left.

When they got home, Kalen helped her unload the groceries. When she tossed him the jerky, he caught it in one big hand. Lainie turned with the scissors just as he ripped the bag open.

He looked at her. "Got it," he said, taking out a few strips before putting the bag away in the pantry.

"I see that." She returned the scissors to the drawer.

The bread dough had risen to the top of the bowl. Lainie punched it down, folded the edges in, and placed it on a lightly floured board. She kneaded it a couple of times then divided it and shaped it into two loaves. Bread was her weakness after chocolate. And wine.

She covered both loaves to let them rise again before baking.

Brennon came into the kitchen, dragging his feet. "Thanks for letting me sleep in," he said, reaching in the fridge for OJ. "It felt great."

"Good."

Lainie prepared the fruit in a bowl, covered it, and placed it in the refrigerator. That would allow the flavors to mix, and she'd add the sweet ingredients in the morning before they left for her mom and dad's house.

"I picked up some beef jerky. Kalen wanted some, so I thought you'd like some, too. It's in the pantry."

"Thanks." He opened the pantry, then took the jerky out.

Jenna strolled in. Fully dressed, with her hair fixed in French braids, it was obvious she'd been up playing around in her room for a while.

"Don't forget you guys need to pack a travel bag to stay the weekend at Gramma and Grampa's," Lainie said.

"I'm already packed," Jenna said.

"Wow, you *are* with-it this morning."

"You know it." Smiling, she dug in the freezer, probably for a toaster waffle.

She was also in a good mood. Lainie loved that.

Kalen grabbed a seat on the other side of the counter, instantly engrossed in the computer.

Lainie pre-heated the oven. When it was ready, she put the bread in to bake.

With everyone chilling today, it was almost impossible to believe she'd fought with a goblin on Monday. But the memory lingered at the edges of her mind.

The house quickly filled with the aroma of baking bread. It seemed homey and warm.

Lainie's phone chimed, and she checked the caller ID. It was her lawyer. Her throat tightened as she answered. Lainie was surprised Nicole Norman was working the day before Thanksgiving.

Lainie answered. "Hello."

"Hi, Lainie. I didn't know whether you'd be home or traveling for the holiday."

"I'll be going to my parent's tomorrow. How about you?"

"We're having my sister and her husband over." There was a slight pause that tugged on Lainie's nerves. "I called because I thought you'd like to know that I received the paperwork today. Your divorce will most likely be final by next week."

Over the phone, Lainie said, "Great." But inside she was jumping up and down.

"You have to work out a shared visitation schedule with him. If that goes well, this will stay out of court."

"Okay. I'll do my part."

"Good. Then call me if you have any problems. I hope you have a nice Thanksgiving."

"Happy Thanksgiving to you also. Bye." Relief flooded Lainie as she disconnected. She would soon be a free woman at last. She smiled.

Brennon and Jenna noticed her cheerful mood. "What's with you?" Brennon asked.

Lainie shrugged. She'd tell them when she actually got the paperwork. It wasn't something she felt compelled to celebrate with her children. That seemed insensitive to their feelings. "I love Thanksgiving." Which was true. She had much to be thankful for.

CHAPTER NINE

Inclusion For The Win

LAINIE'S NERVES SKIPPED ALL over the place as she loaded the car for the day. She had second thoughts about taking Kalen to a family gathering. It occurred to her that she may have to run interference with him throughout the day.

Could she trust him to be alone with her siblings? Had she prepared him enough? What would he accidentally say to her family? She already felt in the spotlight due to her divorce. She didn't need to add complications from Kalen acting weird or something.

But it was too late to change her mind. She'd already told her parents he was coming, and Kalen seemed to be looking forward to the day.

Lainie loaded the bread and ambrosia in the back of the van along with Brennon's and Jenna's overnight bags.

"Time to go," she told them.

Kalen rode up front. Since they'd gone to the store the other day, he knew the drill with the seat belt. The kids sat in the back bucket seats. "Are the animals situated for the day?"

"Yes, I fed Chinchy and Sawyer, and fed and let out Bitsy," Brennon said.

"Good. Thank you." She started the ignition, then tapped her parents' address into the van's GPS. She knew how to get there, but she liked the time clock for arrival. The trip would take an hour and five minutes. Putting the van in gear, she backed out of the driveway,

Lainie had the timepiece tucked inside her pocket. They had not packed their swords. It seemed crazy to do so, not to mention difficult to explain. She hoped they wouldn't need them. She'd also tucked the box into her carry bag in the back. It occurred to her that it might also be a target for the magical community. Now that she had it in her possession, she didn't want to chance losing it.

The drive to Merritt Island was quiet with the kids on their cell phones and Kalen looking out the window.

Lainie broke the silence. "My brothers and the older cousins like to play football after dinner. You can choose to join in or not. They mainly just throw the ball around. Have you watched football games on TV?"

"Yes. I watched Monday Night Football the other night, while you were teaching your dance classes."

"Good. Then you'll know some of what's going on."

Lainie ran down some information about her family to give Kalen more time to absorb it. She'd mentioned it to him before, but with her family, it was a lot to take in. "My mom's name is Janet. My dad is Burt. Crystal is my older sister. She's the oldest of the bunch. I'm the youngest. Crystal is married to Bruce, and they have two children, Tyler and Trevor. Then there are my brothers. Matt's the oldest. His wife is Glenda, and their children are Zoe and Andy. Robbie is in the middle. His wife is Lexi. Their kids are Kevin and Sandra. Anthony is the youngest. Everyone calls him Tony except for my mom. His wife is Mandie, and their kids are Hannah and Billy."

"I'm sure it will be easier to remember them when I have faces to put with the names," Kalen said.

"That's true."

Lainie got off the highway and turned onto the lazy lane her parents lived on, South Tropical Trail. It was an old road, traveling a slice of land that sat between two rivers. Elegant five-acre estates lined the left of the thoroughfare, stretching to the river behind them. The Indian River Lagoon, an intracoastal waterway, offered a serene view to the west. On the east sat the Banana River dotted with docks along the way, sporting a variety of boats. Every now and then, she passed a comparatively dated home—as was her parents'—tucked among the newer pricey ones. Many of the homes were set back well off the road, at the end of winding driveways, hidden by a thick overgrowth of vegetation. She turned onto one such driveway.

She found her parents on the back porch lazily sitting on a swing bench, watching the sunlight swirl and dance across the river as they often did. Two boats traveled by. The aroma of turkey in the oven wafted outside from the kitchen. Lainie was the first of the kids to arrive. She planned it that way. She liked helping her mom get everything set up before the others arrived.

Her mom immediately rose as her grandchildren rounded the corner and met Brennon and Jenna halfway to the door. "Hello, my darlings." She hugged them both to her as if her arms could hold a dozen children within them.

"Something smells good," Brennon said.

"It's Thanksgiving. Of course, it smells delicious."

Grampa chimed in, also rising. "Was the traffic bad coming over?" he asked Lainie.

"About the usual. Too many trucks."

"I know you children must be starved. There are a few things inside to snack on until dinner," her mother said with a smile. "Wash up first."

As soon as Brennon and Jenna ran off to the bathroom, the proverbial pregnant pause made an appearance. Neither of her parents wanted to broach the subject of her divorce, and she'd only said on the phone that she'd fill them in when she got there.

Lainie glanced from her dad to her mom. "I got word yesterday that the divorce is almost final. We're doing really well. So much so, that I can repay you the money you loaned me."

Her mom's face showed doubt. "You don't have to do that, honey."

"I know. But I'm able to. And tomorrow, a realtor friend and I are looking at some properties and a house. I've had a few lucky breaks lately."

Her parents turned their attention from Lainie to Kalen. "And you must be Lainie's friend. I'm Janet, and this is Burt."

"Yes, ma'am. I'm Kalen. I'm pleased to meet you both." He extended his hand.

Janet took his large hand in both of hers and shook it. Burt did the same.

"Would you like something to drink?" Burt asked.

"Yes, thank you." Kalen paused, looking at Lainie. "Would you like anything?" he asked her.

"A glass of tea would be great." While the guys went to get drinks, Lainie unloaded the bread and ambrosia. "I'll be right back," she said to her mom.

She opened the back of the van and took out bread and salad.

"You have a new van," her mom exclaimed. "Very nice! You must be doing well."

"I told you I was. Can you get the door for me?"

She headed straight for the kitchen, then placed the ambrosia in the refrigerator and set the bread on the counter. "Okay. What do you need help with?"

Her mom was the picture of efficiency. The tables were already strung together in a path out onto the porch, set for twenty-three. Tablecloths and Thanksgiving decorations were in place, along with the silverware, metallic-gold charger plates, and napkins. The dinner plates were stacked on the counter since they would be serving buffet style.

Brennon and Jenna wandered into the kitchen, snagging some carrots and dip from the relish tray. "Jenna, how about you help your mom arrange the horn-of-plenty? And Brennon, why don't you give Kalen a tour of the property?"

Leave it to her mom to get everyone settled. Lainie and Jenna assembled the fruits, vegetables, and mixed nuts in an arrangement that spilled out of the horn-of-plenty, down the head table. This was an important display for Lainie's mom. It symbolized all the things they had to be thankful for.

"Done. Now what? How about the drink table?" Lainie asked.

The sound of cars pulling up to the house drifted in through the front door. The others would arrive one after the other. *Let the hoopla begin.*

Lainie set out the cups, ice, and tea. Anyone bringing another drink selection could add it to the side-table.

Her siblings and their families began to file in with hugs, laughter, and kisses. After hugging Janet, they migrated to the back porch and found Burt. Lainie could hear Brennon introducing Kalen to everyone. The cousins divided up into groups. The girls were in the living room and the boys outside at the dock.

"Are you doing okay?" Tony asked, steering her off to the side.

"I'm doing fantastic."

"Well, you look great." He stepped back to get a good look. "I'm glad you're happy. But if you need anything, you come to me. Okay?

We're family, and family helps one another." He gave her a big brotherly hug.

"I know. Thanks. I'm good."

The word was passed along that her dad needed to come carve the turkey. All the dishes were set out. Burt made quick work of the cutting, having many, many years of practice.

"Find a seat everyone and gather round," Janet prompted.

Lainie guided Kalen to sit beside her. Brennon and Jenna found places with the cousins. A low rumble of chatter ensued until Burt gave his famous whistle, then everyone grew quiet.

Her dad said grace and shouted a hearty, "Let's eat."

Lainie's heart swelled as she swallowed the lump in her throat. This is what she loved most. She adored spending time with her large, noisy family.

Everyone progressed single file around the kitchen counter, filling their plates with Thanksgiving fare. Kalen moved along with the group. He seemed quite overwhelmed, his eyes darting from one of her brothers to the next as Matt sent a roll sailing over the heads of others at the table to be deftly caught by Tony. They could be a rowdy bunch, but Lainie smiled.

For a few minutes, the group grew quiet as everyone settled into eating. Slowly, the conversation picked up again. "Kalen, do you have anything like Thanksgiving in Ireland?" Matt asked.

"Like this? No. Our biggest celebration is St. Patrick's Day. It originally celebrated the Catholic St. Patrick who brought Christianity to Ireland."

"Yes. We celebrate St. Patrick's Day also," Matt said.

"Do you?" Kalen asked.

"Yes. It's a popular March holiday," Matt said, shooting Kalen an odd look. Like he thought the guy was pulling his leg.

Lainie knew otherwise. Kalen may not realize the popularity of the holiday here in the US. She suddenly turned nervous that her brother would be able to sniff out that something was off with Kalen.

"Pass me a roll, please," she said, hoping to distract him.

He reached for the basket, then handed it to her. Her ploy seemed to have worked. His attention shifted to something Tony had said about a Christmas gathering. "So you're hosting the family Christmas?" Matt asked Tony.

"I didn't say that," Tony chuckled. His eyes pleaded with his wife on his right. The two had a silent conversation, one that could only pass between a husband and wife, where she was clearly saying 'no.' "We're going to have some work done to the house. It's not a good year for us to host," he said.

"Yeah, Yeah," Chrystal ribbed him. "I hosted last year. So who's up?"

Tony gave her a warning look.

Lainie paused in chewing a bite of turkey. Her desire to throw her hat in to host the holiday gathering was almost uncontrollable. She slowly finished the bite and swallowed, the idea vibrating through her. In all her adult years, all the years she'd been married to John, she'd never hosted the gathering. Their home hadn't been large enough for the entire family. John had been adamantly against making any sort of arrangements, like having it at the church or park in order for her to take her turn. It had been one more thing that was like a thorn in her flesh.

For several minutes, everyone seemed once again engrossed in eating, but most plates were almost clean, so eating didn't seem like the reason for the silence. She knew her brothers' hesitation came from their wives. A gathering meant work.

Lainie worried her lower lip. For once, money, or the lack of it, wasn't a problem for her. She could come up with a plan, couldn't she? She gulped a fortifying breath of air.

"I'll host the holiday party," she said with a nervous giggle. They usually selected a weekend date after Christmas to gather. "I'll let everyone know the details next week."

"Lainie, you don't have to do that. You're just getting on your feet after the divorce," Robbie said.

Humph. He hadn't said a word until now. "I'm doing great," Lainie said. "I *want* to do this." Then she stared at Crystal. "I need to do this."

Her sister got the message that Lainie had made up her mind. "Okay, then. That's settled. Lainie will host the family Christmas gathering. And if you need anything, just give me a yell," Crystal said.

Her brothers nodded, getting the message. "Okay. Just let us know the date," Robbie said.

"I will," Lainie said, unsure if what she'd done was wise but feeling giddy that she'd taken it on.

After dinner, pie, and sitting around too full to move, the guys and kids and the one athletic sister-in-law went outside on the lawn and played the annual football game. Kalen joined them. Lainie helped her mom clean up along with the help of Crystal and sisters-in-law Lexi and Glenda.

After they'd finished, they sat on the porch and visited while her brothers took turns taking people for boat rides. Around four in the afternoon, everyone slowly packed up and left. Lainie gave Brennon and Jenna the customary instructions to behave and help their grandparents.

She was the first sibling to arrive and the second one to depart. As wonderful as it was to gather together, it was also emotionally exhausting.

This year had been different without John. The dynamics were different, too, because he had never gotten along that well with her brothers. Today, she'd felt like everyone was watching her to make sure she was okay, looking for any sign of a breakdown, despite her telling them otherwise.

Her mom handed her a large to-go plate of leftovers, another Thanksgiving tradition. She needed to eat turkey sandwiches at least through the weekend. Her mom hugged her goodbye. "I put plenty of extra in there since you have a house guest. We'll bring the kids home Sunday afternoon. Is that okay?"

"Yes. That's fine. I'll see you then. Thank you for everything." She squeezed her mom's shoulders.

And behind it all, Lainie had the niggling feeling something else was about to change.

CHAPTER TEN

I'd Rather Sleep Than Go Out

BLACK FRIDAY. WHILE EVERYONE else got up early to frantically shop for the best Christmas deals, Lainie sat on the porch, glued to her computer, researching vineyards. What did it take to own one? What did it take to run one? What were her chances of succeeding?

She examined the vineyard she was considering purchasing. Then she studied ones already operating across the country in California, Washington, Nebraska, and West Virginia.

Based on her research, she constructed her list of what she thought she'd need. That way, she could talk to the present owner with some knowledge in place. She didn't know who he had in place already, but to make it a solid operation, she'd need a CFO, operations manager, winemaker, and events and marketing director. As the owner, she would oversee it all. The idea was both exciting and daunting. It would be great if Alaina and Karen wanted to invest in the winery, but she wanted them as investors only, not part owners. With that, she needed to speak to a lawyer before making any deals.

Sure, they were her friends, but the bottom line was that she wanted the winery to be hers. They already had their chosen jobs. She'd had no career, except dance. This was her chance.

They would arrive shortly to pick her up, so she needed to decide how to handle this.

The doorbell rang. Bitsy went nuts barking. She wondered if Alaina and Karen had ridden together again. Probably. She closed the computer. *Humph*. They'd probably come to the door instead of texting from the car because Alaina wanted another look at Kalen.

Lainie laughed at the idea as she answered the door. Kalen lounged on the couch watching TV.

She was immediately shoved backward, realizing too late that she should have looked to see who it was first. But she was expecting her friends.

Instead, a man pushed into the room, forcing her back. Blinking, she sucked in a ragged breath. She recognized him.

Kalen jumped up, turning.

"It's the guy I saw when we were at Sam's last week," Lainie said.

The guy bared his teeth at her.

"Get out," she screamed at him. The man grabbed at her, like he was trying to get to her pockets. He must have sensed where the timepiece was. He kept reaching for her, and she continued to bat his arm away.

Kalen planted one big foot on the sofa and jumped over it, landing to stand next to her. He stared at the man. "He's a werewolf," Kalen said. "They have shifting magic similar to dragons. But they're devious and corrupt."

Behind her, Lainie heard a scampering of tiny feet. She glanced to the side to see Sawyer and Chinchy.

"Dragon, get out of my way," the wolf man ordered.

As if he didn't care about Kalen, the wolf man lunged toward Lainie. "I know you have the timepiece. Its power is calling me."

Anger flashed in Kalen's eyes. With a swipe of his arm, he thrust the guy back.

Lainie drew the watch from her pocket. It had knocked John back that time in the parking lot; perhaps she could use it against wolf man.

She extended her arm out and flipped open the timepiece, trying to recall what she'd done before to engage the watch. She concentrated.

Take him out. Hit him. Punch him.

Nothing.

She wasn't directing the magic — she was *pushing* at it the way she swung a sword, using brute force instead of controlled intention. Clearly, she needed training in how the timepiece responded.

Behind the guy, Alaina and Karen advanced up the walk. "What's going on?" Karen demanded.

With shocking speed, the guy grabbed hold of Karen's wrist and whirled her in front of his chest. Alaina lifted her purse to strike the guy over his head, but he sidestepped, so her arm dropped through the air.

Wolf guy reached into his pocket, withdrew a gun, and held it at Karen's head.

"Oh jeez," Lainie whispered.

"Give me the timepiece, or I start shooting," he warned.

She glanced at Kalen. If only they had their swords. But she had propped them in the corner.

"Get in here," Kalen said to Alaina.

She scooted past the threshold, inching closer to Lainie.

Lainie closed the watch and held the timepiece up by the chain, letting it dangle, hoping to entice wolf man to let his guard down so Kalen could jump him. The talisman spun, seeming to gain speed. Wolf man bobbed his gun at Lainie. "Hand it over." It turned round and round. A whistling sound formed, sounding like the rush of wind through an ally. It grew louder and louder, like a hurricane-force wind whipped up and blew very fast. The roar echoed in the room. She felt the wind pushing her, pushing her. There was a boom and a flash of light. Across the room, a space opened.

At a loud crack—for an instant, she'd thought he'd fired the gun, but no—a slit of light glowed like a door at the end of a long corridor.

Bitsy barked.

Lainie sucked in a breath. "What is it?" She spoke more to herself than to the others.

"A portal to another dimension," Sawyer said.

"The timepiece must have opened it," Lainie whispered.

"No," wolf man wailed, aiming the gun at her. He swayed, still holding Karen. This time, it was the gun that went off, but he missed her. Lainie inhaled sharply. She couldn't, wouldn't allow him to hurt her friends. He was here because of the timepiece. This was her fault. Terror held her rooted in place. How could she win against a gun?

Urgently, Sawyer yelled, "Step through. Everyone, step through."

The roar echoed in the room. She felt the wind pushing her, pushing her—

she hadn't meant to open anything.

Which terrified her more than the werewolf did. At once, Lainie felt as if she'd been pushed. She grabbed hold of Karen's arm as she leaped forward, into the portal, hoping to escape the wolf with the gun. Kalen scrambled toward the man, and then a tumble of bodies joined her. She thought she heard a howl.

When they stopped falling, she discovered they were on a swing-bridge. They stood holding the metal rails. Alaina and Karen were right next to her, breathing hard. Thank heavens they were okay. Kalen arrived behind them, Sawyer at his feet and Chinchy on his shoulder, with a blade in each hand. And behind them was black nothingness. No portal into her house. Nothing.

Lainie waited a moment to allow her eyes to adjust and her heart to stop pounding in her ears. She needed to think.

"Where are we?" Karen asked.

"I'm not sure," Lainie said.

"We're at the entrance of another dimension," Sawyer provided. "The bridge links the portals to the two worlds."

"I don't want to go to another dimension," Lainie said frantically. "My children are back there."

"And they are safe," Sawyer said.

Karen and Alaina exchanged a nervous look.

"The cat talks," Karen said, leaning close to Lainie.

"Well, yes," Lainie answered. "I'll explain later."

"Do what you did with the watch again," Kalen said. "Maybe it will open back up."

Lainie held up the watch by its chain, letting it spin. She waited. They all waited, eyeing the direction from which they came.

No opening appeared.

She tried again, this time starting the spin with her fingers.

A sickly taste filled her mouth. Still, nothing. Except for the light in the opposite direction. "We can't stay on the bridge," she said. "Let's go have a look. Maybe there's a way back from there."

Lainie led the way. Kalen brought up the rear. They crossed the bridge toward the sliver of light which grew taller and wider as they approached it. When there was no more bridge, they had no choice but to step through the portal or fall into the blackness beneath them.

Lainie stepped through onto a patch of green grass. The others came behind her, bumping into her. She stumbled to the ground, trying not to feel like this was all her fault.

She stood and looked over her shoulder, taking stock that they were all there, she was stunned and concerned. Alaina and Karen seemed fine. As did Kalen. But the cat and the chinchilla were missing. And they seemed to have gained a golden-haired knight with a sheathed sword at his hip, along with a falcon perched on Kalen's shoulder.

"Where are Chinchy and Sawyer?" Lainie asked. "They didn't fall from the bridge, did they?"

"No, sweetheart. I'm right here. Thank you for your concern." The knight with shoulder-length hair the color of the marmalade cat, tugged at his mail shirt, adjusting it.

"Sawyer? Is that you?" Lainie asked.

"In the flesh."

Lainie's brows dipped together. "Don't scare me like that."

"Where are we going now?" the hawk asked.

Why wasn't she surprised the bird could talk? Major changes had happened all around her when they came through the portal. The vibrant color of the landscape contrasted with the dark bridge of the portal.

"I think I'm going to be ill," Alaina complained.

"Hold on," Kalen said. "How about we stop to rest?"

Lainie led their little band over to a large rock. They all sat, resting, and evaluated their surroundings. She noted immediately that there didn't seem to be a portal back. Where they had come through was closed.

CHAPTER ELEVEN

Where Am I?

"WHAT HAPPENED TO THE werewolf?" Lainie asked.

"He may be missing his gun hand," Kalen said.

She winced. At some point, Kalen had connected with the swords. She suspected that was how wolfie had lost a hand.

"Where are we?" Lainie asked.

"Esidarap. Another dimension," Sawyer said.

"We need to find the way back," Lainie said, her voice urgent. She couldn't remain stuck here. The kids would be coming home from her parents. Not to mention that her friends couldn't simply disappear.

"What is all this?" Karen demanded. "We came to get you and visit a winery, and now we're not even on Earth? This deserves a measure of panic," she said, her voice quivering.

"Hold on and stay strong. We'll figure a way out of this," Lainie said. "The timepiece brought us here, so it should take us back." She stood, holding the talisman in front of her by the chain. The watch started to spin. She waited until it began to slow. Nothing happened. No portal appeared.

Dang it.

With her fingers, she gave the timepiece a twist, causing it to spin faster. It spun and then slowed to a stop, then spun in the opposite direction. Lainie held her breath. Did the direction of the spinning have anything to do with what had happened? *Come on. Open*. She exhaled. *Still no portal*. Her shoulders slumped in defeat.

Maybe raw need wasn't enough. Maybe this required finesse — the same precision Kalen drilled into her sword work. She grimaced. Great. More training.

"Maybe I need to give it some time. I'll try again in a few minutes."

The group, sitting on the rock, nodded in agreement.

Fifteen minutes ticked by, and she tried again to open the portal. *Nope*. She didn't understand why it wouldn't work.

"Okay, we'll get nowhere by sitting here. I need to find Felicity." Lainie stood, taking in her surroundings. Judging by the lay of the land, they seemed to be on a hill or mountainous ground. Perhaps if they began walking, they'd run into someone who could direct them to the portal out of here.

"Let's walk," she said. "There doesn't seem to be anything in the upward direction, so we'll head down."

"That's as good a strategy as any," Sawyer said.

"Wait," Kalen said. "I'll change into my dragon form and fly reconnaissance to look over the area."

"That sounds like a great plan," Lainie said. "You can cover more ground that way. In the meantime, I'll try to summon Felicity. She should know how to get us back through the portal."

"Yes. And I'll get an idea of what direction we should go," Kalen said. "Chinchy can fly with me."

"Okay," Lainie said.

Kalen stepped away from the group. With a huge curl of red-and-gray smoke, he transformed into his dragon form, seeming larger than he had in her bedroom. Perhaps it was because he had room to stretch out. He had huge feet and strong legs to support a massive torso of sleek, shiny scales, each one a work of art in iridescent hues of teals, blues, and greens. He was magnificent with the sunlight shining on him, appearing as if thousands of tiny prism lights sparkled all over his huge, muscular body. His clothes were piled on the grass.

"This won't take long," he said in a deep resonant voice.

"Okay. Be careful." She wasn't sure why she'd said the last.

With a powerful flap of his wings, he launched into the air, his wings carrying him effortlessly into the sky within seconds. He soared in a circle above them, and then took off and was quickly out of sight.

Twin gasps came from behind Lainie. She turned to discover Alaina clutching Karen's arm, like the woman would save her from a horrible beast. Both of her friends looked pale, their eyes wide with disbelief. "Yes, you just saw him change into a dragon," she said. "He came from a paranormal romance book. Did I tell you that? I don't remember." She shook her head, trying to remember.

Dang it, she hated when she couldn't recall if she'd done something or simply *thought* about doing it.

Lainie picked up Kalen's clothes as well as the two swords he'd been carrying. She handed one of the swords to Sawyer to hold. Kalen would need them when he returned.

Alaina and Karen exchanged a glance, clearly unsure. "Now what?" Karen asked.

"We wait until he returns. But not out in the middle of the field. Let's move to the stand of trees."

"Sounds good to me," Alaina said. "In the movies, they always take cover."

"Unfortunately, this isn't a movie," Karen said.

"I know. But that's the only source of knowledge I can draw on about this situation," Alaina replied.

"It will be fine," Lainie added with her usual positive response. "The timepiece will get us back to our time."

Sawyer gave a disbelieving chuckle. "As soon as you figure out how it works."

Lainie pressed her lips together. "Let's go."

They all followed Lainie, walking through the grassy field until they came to a path. Paths generally led to places, so Lainie took that turn. She could see they were traveling toward lush green trees and shrubbery ahead. Plus, she could hear water, maybe even a waterfall by the sound of it. Between the trees, at a distance, she could make out buildings.

Then, among the trees, something darted from one tree to the next. She stopped. "Come out," she said. "We're lost and trying to find our way."

There was a shuffle and shake of branches. Lainie paused. "Stay here," she said to the rest of them. She felt like she should approach alone. She walked around a tree. From the other side, she spied a castle below with beautiful spires of gold.

In the green field in front of her, three beautiful white unicorns romped, running back and forth as if playing a game of tag. Light shimmered and danced off their coats with every muscular movement they made. Their manes fluttered in the breeze and glistened like sunbeams in colorful contrast of blues, teals, pinks, and lavender. Then two flying horses, reminding her of Pegasus in Greek mythology, flew in to join them, running along the ground and taking flight again, then circling back.

Suddenly one of the unicorns caught sight of her. The group stopped playing and banded together. As a group, they approached. They were the most gorgeous creatures she'd ever seen. She'd always admired the physique of horses, with their sleek lines, powerful muscles and athletic ability to run like the wind. They were living art forms and the subject of poetry and songs.

The lead unicorn stepped forward. "What are you doing in Esidarap, humans?"

"You can speak?" Lainie asked.

"Of course, we can speak. All the animals in this realm can talk. I've heard that's not the case everywhere."

"No. It's not that way on Earth," Lainie said.

"That's too bad. I'm Simone. So back to my original question—why are you here?"

"We were being chased by a werewolf and fell into a portal to escape him," Karen said. "Is that the gist of it?" Karen asked rapidly, peering at Lainie for confirmation.

"Yes, I'd say so." It seemed Karen didn't have the patience to take it slow.

"Except you left out the part about the gun," Alaina added.

"A gun?" Simone gave a shiver, and the other enchanted horses stepped back as if the word itself could hurt them.

Lainie, Karen, and Alaina exchanged looks of speculation at the flying horse's reaction. Lainie wondered what traumatic past experiences the animals had been through. Had other humans been here? If there was one magical timepiece, it made sense to her that there could be more. Perhaps there were even other ways to get in and out of the realm.

"Have other humans come to Esidarap?" Lainie asked.

"From time to time," Simone said. "Plus, there's a small village of mundane residents, people who choose to live in old-world ways."

"Really?" Lainie didn't think she would want to give up the creature comforts she had at home. But she imagined there were people who would like to step back in time.

"Well, our goal is to get home," Karen said, looking around at the countryside.

"We're looking for the fairy Felicity," Lainie said.

"Ah. It will be more likely she'll find you rather than the other way around," Simone said. "Well, good luck." The unicorn backed up and rejoined the group. She dipped her head as if in a salute goodbye, then she and the others galloped off into the woods.

Almost at the same time, another animal ambled out from among the shrubs. A huge, majestic buck, Lainie realized. She wondered if that had anything to do with Simone's abrupt departure. The buck sported a huge, stunning rack, spanning at least twenty-four inches. He lumbered up to her. "What is it you seek, fair human?"

She held up the timepiece for him to see. "We need to find the portal to get home."

The buck dipped his head and snorted. "I'm known as Brutus. Do you not have a fairy escort? They are responsible for safe passage." At first, Lainie was going to reply no, but then she thought of Felicity. What had she said about don't be a stranger?

"Not at the moment. We're looking for fairy Felicity." She told him the same thing she'd said to Simone.

"It is not safe for you in Esidarap right now. There is a war going on between the fairies and nymphs. The rumor is the nymph ruler is set on revenge. You don't want to get caught in the middle of that."

"No, we don't. We arrived by accident and only want to go home," Alaina said.

Lainie felt horrible for her friends. She had never imagined anything like this could happen. They had to get back home pronto. "I'm sure Felicity will find us and help us."

"I hope you're right," Brutus said. "If not, my home turf is straight back through the brush over there. You're welcome to come find me. I can provide a measure of protection."

"Thank you. That's very kind." Lainie sighed. "I hope we don't need to take you up on your generous offer."

"It's always good to have a backup plan," he said.

"You're absolutely right," Karen chimed in.

Brutus said goodbye and turned back to the woods.

A breeze skimmed over Lainie's arms. Her friends were with her, yet she felt quite alone because this all rested on her shoulders. It was her fault they were here. Her association with the fairy and talisman had brought them here and placed them all in danger of not finding their way back home.

Just as she was feeling her lowest, a gigantic shadow passed overhead. She tilted her head back, peering up. Relief washed over her as Kalen returned.

He alit out in the more open area with control and grace. Again, she marveled at the beauty of his dragon form. He transformed with another wisp of smoke and stood totally naked. Alaina coughed, but neither she nor Karen looked away. It was as if they were in one of those Chip and Dale shows and they were in for all they could see. Lainie cleared her throat.

That got their attention...just barely. She tossed Kalen his clothes. He quickly dressed, then began his report.

"There's a castle not far from here in that direction." He pointed in the same direction she'd seen the castle beyond the woods.

"Yes, I saw it as well."

Given this was another realm, Lainie didn't have a clue what was north, south, east, or west. Or even if those markers were relevant.

"I believe we should travel there. It would seem a likely place for the fairy you seek," Kalen said. "Also, there's a band of creatures, taking what appears to be a battle stance, in my estimation, over the ridge that way." He pointed in the opposite direction. "They're perhaps a day's march away."

"Brutus mentioned that the fairies and nymphs were at war. Maybe they're planning a strike on the castle," Lainie said.

"It could be," Kalen remarked.

"When we see Felicity we should warn her," Lainie said.

"Should we get involved in this?" Karen asked. "We know nothing about this world."

"That's true. But war is war, and if I can help protect innocent lives, then I will," Lainie said. She wondered what the nymph ruler was exacting revenge for.

They walked in the direction Kalen had indicated for a mile or so, until he stopped. "There," he said, pointing.

Lainie peered between the trees, seeing the castle below with paths and waterfalls. She motioned for her group to come closer, showing Karen, Alaina, and Sawyer the splendor before them. "We may have to go into the castle."

She paused and thought.

Pulling out the timepiece, she cupped it in front of her, recalling the way she'd brought the fairy to her. She turned it so the fairy on the timepiece faced skyward and placed her thumbs over the jewels of her wings. She pressed and held them like that, connecting all the stones.

The fairy Felicity didn't show. Lainie's heart sank. She had been hoping that would have worked. Maybe Felicity only came when she was in Earth realm. Lainie prayed that wasn't the case. She needed Felicity now, in this realm.

They traipsed onward, between the trees, and walked alongside a stream, continuing in the direction of the castle.

Out of the woods on the opposite side of the stream, a fairy marched, carrying a bow at her side. She was dressed in white, the tips of her pointy ears peeking through her blonde hair. Felicity.

She flew over the stream, then halted near Lainie. "What do you want?" she asked irritably.

"I want to go home. We fell into this dimension, and we can't get back."

Felicity nodded. She raised her bow, notched an arrow, and let it fly. Lainie thought she heard it hit its mark, but she wasn't sure. "We're at war at the moment. Bring your group together, and I'll open the portal."

Lainie's heart thumped wildly in her chest. Yes, that was precisely what they needed. She waved to the group. They were standing several yards behind her, but they came running.

"Gather together," Felicity said. "The portal can only be seen from a certain angle. You have to be in that line of sight."

Felicity waved her hand, and a portal opened. "Travel across the bridge. Don't stop."

Lainie absorbed the way Felicity's fingers moved, the ripple in the air. If portals could be opened on purpose...it meant they could be *learned*.

"Okay. Thank you."

Felicity notched another arrow. "Now go."

Lainie made a beeline straight across the bridge to the other side. She glanced over her shoulder to find her group right behind her. On the far side of the bridge, the portal door opened into her home. She stepped through, dragging the others with her. Kalen came last, and the portal closed.

They all tumbled into her foyer, amazed by what had happened and the new knowledge they had of another dimension.

Lainie noted the splatters of blood on the tile and out the front door. It seemed Wolfie had left after his confrontation with Kalen. The drops on the tile were the only evidence the werewolf had been in the house. There was no sign of it now.

The creature had attacked them in her home. Anger swelled inside her. How dare he? The reality of what they'd been through slammed into her. What if they hadn't made it back home? What if the bullet had hit its mark? What if Felicity hadn't come to her?

Part of her wanted to explode into a rant. She reined in her emotions, feeling the heat in her face. The next creature wouldn't wait for her to catch up — she needed her mind as sharp as her sword

"Are you all right?" Kalen asked, watching her intently.

"Yes. I'm just...tired." And furious, pissed, scared, and thankful for being home.

Emotionally exhausted, they stumbled into the living room and dropped onto the sofa and chairs. "I don't want to go through that again," Alaina said.

"Me, either." Karen pinned Lainie with a stare. "But I'd love to hear all about your adventures leading up to this, Lainie. You obviously have something to share."

"After we're revived by a little nourishment. And by nourishment, I mean chocolate. My energy has been sucked right out of me," Lainie groaned.

She glanced around. Sawyer and Chinchy were back to their normal forms.

"Are we still going to the vineyard," Lainie asked. "After we recover, of course."

Karen rolled her eyes. "What time is it? How long have we been gone? I need to rest a minute."

Lainie stood, walked to the kitchen, then retrieved a bag of Dove chocolates. She returned passing them out. "Here you go. Fairy food."

CHAPTER TWELVE

Everything Hurts

Anyone want a glass of wine?" Lainie asked as she went back into the kitchen. It was the middle of the day, but given what they'd just been through, they deserved something to relax them.

"Me," Karen said.

"Sure," Alaina chimed in.

"I'll also join you," Kalen added, walking into the kitchen to help.

Lainie pulled four glasses from the cabinet and handed them to Kalen who took them out to the living room. After opening a bottle of red, she poured everyone a glass, then, with a groan acknowledging her still-aching muscles, she plopped onto the sofa next to Alaina. They all sat there for several long, silent moments before succumbing to the temptation of chocolate. A perfect pairing for the wine.

"So, spill," Karen said finally. "How did all this come about?"

Lainie supposed that, after all they had been through, they deserved an explanation. "Let me first point out that while we were gone, time seemed to stand still here. So basically, we're right back where we started with regards to my living situation. And we can still head out to the winery."

"All right. But first..." Karen pinned her with a demanding gaze.

"Years ago, I received a pocket watch from my grandmother. I'd forgotten all about it until I found it in my closet the night I was packing to... to leave John." She hadn't thought of that night for a few weeks, and realized it still felt surreal to think of all that had happened since that night. Since finding the timepiece. "Well, it turned out to be magical, and there are other creatures who would like to possess it. I'm sorry you both got caught in the middle of it."

"And the talking cat and shifting dragon?" Alaina asked.

Lainie shrugged. "The timepiece conjured those. Along with money that's been magically appearing in my purse every day since I brought the talisman home. Large amounts of money. I can almost afford the vineyard on my own," she admitted.

"Wow. Just wow," Karen said.

"I know. Pretty crazy. If it weren't happening to me, I wouldn't believe it," Lainie said, then sobered. "But, as I've come to realize, magic doesn't happen without a price. These other magical creatures are after the talisman and its power."

"Like the werewolf earlier," Alaina said.

"Yes."

"And what if the price is too high?" Karen asked.

Lainie wouldn't allow that to happen. "Oh hush. Don't give me any negative crap. It's important to stay positive."

Alaina leaned in, lowering her voice. "Well, I'd take the dragon-shifter perk any day." She winked.

"Yeah. He's growing on me," Lainie admitted, glancing into the kitchen.

Kalen was digging through the refrigerator, evidently wine and chocolate weren't enough for him. And it probably wasn't enough for the rest of them, either. It was approaching lunchtime. They should take a little time to recover from their adventure. "I have plenty of leftovers from Thanksgiving. Anyone want a turkey sandwich?"

"Sure," Alaina said, standing. "I love leftover turkey, but since I don't have a large family, I usually volunteer at the local food-sharing center, dishing out meals."

"That's very nice of you," Lainie said.

Alaina shrugged one shoulder. "I've done it ever since the divorce."

"I'll take a sandwich, also," Karen said.

Everyone gathered in the kitchen around the island. Lainie set out the leftover turkey and sandwich fixings along with a stack of paper plates. "Help yourselves."

She offered Sawyer a small slice of turkey. He gobbled up. "Thanks."

As Lainie fixed Kalen's sandwich, she recalled the first time he had eaten one and how he'd found it a novelty that he'd not had before. Once they'd all prepared their sandwiches, they sat at the counter to eat.

"I can't believe I was just in another dimension. It all seems *Twilight Zone*-ish," Karen said.

"Now there's an old TV show," Alaina commented.

"What's that?" Kalen asked.

Lainie liked that Kalen felt comfortable enough around this group for him to ask. "It's a TV show that was on when I was a kid where they featured odd and unimaginable occurrences," Karen explained. "Like when people went into a certain swimming pool, never to be seen again, with no explanation for it."

Kalen raised his brows. "That is strange."

"The stories weren't real even though they tried to pass them off as authentic. They still gave me the creeps." Lainie shivered. She washed down the last of her sandwich with iced tea.

"Well, I didn't think a realm of fairies and talking animals was real until today," Alaina said.

"By the way, how are we going to handle this with the other gals, Picku, Nandita, and Shreena? Do we keep it secret or share with them our amazing adventure?" Karen asked.

"So now, it's an amazing adventure?" Lainie teased.

"It's usually amazing once the danger is over," Karen retorted. "We're home safe and sound."

Lainie chuckled. When everyone had finished their lunch, Lainie cleared the counter, putting everything away. "Okay, who's ready to go to the winery?"

"I don't know," Alaina said. "After this morning, I may need some recovery time."

"Lainie only has this rental for two more weeks," Karen said. She either has to find a place or a new rental." She turned her attention to Lainie. "Right?"

Lainie nodded. "Right."

"I'll go," Kalen announced.

Lainie blinked. She hadn't meant to include him. Karen and Alaina seemed to enjoy his company, though. After the way he helped them in the fairy realm, he could act like her bodyguard. Since the werewolf had attacked them, having him along might be a good idea. And given how hard he'd been trying to fit in and be helpful, she should be more open to including him. After all, it didn't look like she'd be sending him back into the book any time soon.

"You can be our bodyguard," Lainie half-joked.

He reached for his sword.

"You'll have to find something smaller than that to carry," Lainie said.

Kalen nodded. "No problem." He went upstairs, then returned several minutes later. Lainie didn't know what weapon he'd chosen because it was concealed.

He held his hands up and turned around. All Lainie could think was, *Damn he looks good*. She wanted to feel the stubble on his chin, run her fingers through his hair, and press her lips against his.

"Is this okay?" he asked.

She knew he meant that there wasn't a weapon showing, but her mind, well, it went where it wanted. And there was just something about him that drew her in.

"Yes. I don't see anything that will attract undue attention." Except for the man himself. He was extremely noticeable. Heads turned when he walked by.

"Do you think we're still in danger?" Karen asked.

Lainie skirted the question. "I don't know, but better safe than sorry." Since there had already been three attempts made to take the timepiece, she figured more would follow. The werewolf encounter had been the scariest of all. Perhaps she should have simply handed over the talisman.

Strange, she finally felt like she had something of her own, something undeniably special. Now, she desperately wanted to keep it. Short of putting her family and friends in danger, she planned to do just that.

Lainie blew out a breath of annoyance. *Come back down to earth, Lainie girl*. "We better get going if we're going to the vineyard," she said.

"Okay," Alaina said, reluctantly. "I feel better now that I've eaten and put our little journey behind us."

"Right," Karen agreed.

Lainie picked up her purse and keys from the counter. "I'll drive."

"Let me call the seller and tell him we're on our way," Karen said, stepping into her realtor shoes.

"Sounds good."

Karen sat in the passenger seat, and Kalen and Alaina took the back seats. Lainie's van was much roomier than Karen's smaller car, which was part of the reason she'd suggested it now that Kalen was coming with them. That meant she and Kalen didn't have to share a back seat.

As she got closer to the vineyard, she felt the urge to hum or sing. The idea of buying the place pleased her to no end. She told herself to cool it, that she'd end up disappointed if the guy didn't sell it to her, or if something else got in the way of the sale. Still, a happy tune continued in her head.

Lainie turned into the long drive leading to the house, parked, and they all got out. As she strolled to the front door, she reached into her purse and touched the timepiece. She couldn't believe how much she wanted this. It was beyond her wildest dreams.

Charles Lambert must have heard them pull up, because he opened the door before they got to the porch. He smiled warmly. "Welcome. I knew you'd be back. I felt it the other day when you were here."

"Mr. Lambert, I—" Lainie began.

"Would like to make you a counteroffer," Karen interrupted, eyeing Lainie.

"We're talking about a lot of money," Lainie said. "We'd like to negotiate a deal."

"Please, call me Charlie. You're going to buy this place. I saw it in a dream," Mr. Lambert said. "And there will be weddings." He glanced between Lainie and Kalen.

What was with that? Did he think they were a couple? No way.

Lainie took a deep breath. "If you reduce the price by ten percent, I'll put seventy-percent cash down and finance the remainder through you with the option to pay off the balance without penalty."

Karen eyed Lainie as if to ask, *You have that kind of money?* and then nodded firmly. "That sounds like an excellent proposition."

"Sold," Mr. Lambert said, smiling from ear to ear. "My wife would have been thrilled to know you're the new owner."

"Shall we go inside? I'll make notes of the details," Karen said. "Then I can draw up the contract.

"Certainly." Mr. Lambert stepped aside, indicating for them to enter ahead of him. "Is the living room all right?"

"Yes," Karen said.

"Is it okay if Kalen and I take a walk outside while you do that?" Alaina asked.

"By all means, go ahead. If it's acceptable with the new owner," Charlie said.

"I'm not the new owner yet." Lainie chuckled. "But go ahead. Then we can talk about any ideas later."

An hour later, they had all the fine print ironed out. Karen was fast and efficient. She would have the contract for them to sign within a week, at which time the monies would be exchanged for the turnkey deal. Lainie would purchase the house and vineyard furnished, Charlie would occupy the guesthouse for thirty days to help with the transition of the winery operation. All the staff had the option of staying on and would be encouraged to do so.

Plus, the first wedding would be held just before Christmas in a few weeks. It seemed Charlie's wife had wanted to dabble in expanding into a destination wedding venue, and his niece was scheduled to be the first bride to say "I do" on the property. Charlie assured them that they didn't have to do a thing because a wedding planner was handling everything. All they had to do was provide the venue.

After they had finished their discussions, Lainie stood at the huge panel windows, looking out at the backyard and small lake. She felt like she should pinch herself. Was all this actually hers?

Was this real? Would she wake tomorrow to find everything had been a dream? Or a vision of the timepiece? Would she be reverted to the trailer and old van at the stroke of midnight like the pumpkin and carriage in the *Cinderella* story?

No. This wasn't the same at all.

Lainie's stomach fluttered with anticipation. She could feel the power of the timepiece bolstering her emotionally and magically.

Alaina and Kalen stood near the lake. Alaina placed a hand on his shoulder, laughing. A foreign emotion laced through Lainie. A small part of her didn't like the closeness between her friend and her... What was Kalen to her? Protector, according to Felicity.

"I'll call you when the papers are ready, We'll meet in my office since I have a notary available. We'll have everything we need to complete the transaction," Karen said from behind her.

Lainie turned. "Thank you so much, Charlie." Lainie held out her hand, and he took it in both of his and shook it.

"I feel like I've done more than sell my property," he said. "But time will tell if I'm right."

She wasn't sure what he was referring to.

Alaina and Kalen strolled in through the kitchen door. "How's it going?" Alaina asked.

"All finished," Karen said with a smile.

Lainie's eyes met Kalen's. He gave her a wink with a tilt of his chin. Her heart leaped in her chest. *No, no, no.*

After everyone loaded into the van, Lainie waved at Charlie as they drove away. If everything went well, she'd be moving in here soon.

CHAPTER THIRTEEN

Perfectly Fine With Who We Are

KAREN AND ALAINA WERE exceptionally chatty on the way back. They were already suggesting a wine gathering with the girls at Lainie's new house.

"And maybe you can have some fun with your magical timepiece," Alaina said.

"It's not a toy," Lainie reminded them.

"I know, but from what you've told me, it gave you some yummy things," Alaina said from the back seat. She paused a bit too long, making Lainie uncomfortable. "Like how many desserts have you conjured up?"

"I'm still learning how it works," Lainie confessed.

"Lainie is correct. What is the saying I heard on the TV? If you play with fire you're going to get burned," Kalen said.

"Mmm, burn me," Alaina teased. "Wait. Forget I said that."

"What have you been drinking?" Karen joked.

"It's the winery. It's gone to my head." Alaina giggled.

Something had went to her head, but Lainie didn't think it was the winery.

When they got to Lainie's house, Karen and Alaina transferred to Karen's car. "I'll call you as soon as I have the contracts done," Karen said out her car window.

"Super. I can't wait."

It was three-thirty in the afternoon, when she and Kalen both collapsed on the sofa in the living room. Lainie hadn't done a speck of Black Friday shopping, but she felt as if she'd charged through a slew of stores, scouring them for Christmas deals. She did not enjoy shopping because she rarely had money to spend. Although Christmas was different. She'd always used the money she made teaching dance classes to make the holiday special for the kids.

The joy on their faces on Christmas morning meant everything to her. It was worth the hours of coupon-saving and discount-shopping.

Lainie couldn't believe that this year would be different. She could buy the kids whatever they wanted for Christmas. She'd count the vineyard as a present to herself. A new beginning in a new life.

All thanks to the magical timepiece.

Though exhausted, she was still keyed up from the day's events. That evil werewolf trying to force her to give up the talisman, discovering the portal, and then the excitement of making an offer on the winery and house.

Kalen turned on the TV. His fascination with it had steadily grown. The sound of a program overtook her thoughts. She closed her eyes, relaxing a little as the tension in her neck and shoulders eased. *Mmm.*

The next thing she knew, she was resting on the sofa with her feet in Kalen's lap. She must have fallen asleep. She jerked, trying to sit up.

"You're fine. Just stay put," Kalen said. "There's no hurry to get up."

Easy for him to say. She shouldn't be lounging with any part of her touching his lap.

"What time is it?"

"Eight o'clock."

"Oh jeez. I've been sleeping for hours. You should have woken me."

"You must have needed the rest."

Kalen massaged her feet, first one foot then the other. Glorious sensations swept through her, making her entire body even more relaxed. Even more reluctant to move and get up. She moaned.

"Are you hungry?"

Her eyes flew open. Um, yeah, she was hungry for more of his divine touch, more of—wrong answer. She swung her legs to the side and away from him as she sat up. The room swirled off-kilter. Maybe she'd done that too fast.

"I can fix us an omelet for dinner," Kalen offered.

"That sounds surprisingly delicious," she muttered.

Kalen stood and ambled into the kitchen. He seemed to be adapting quite well to this time period. She stayed on the sofa for several long moments, tuning into the sounds in the kitchen, the refrigerator opening and closing, the scrape of a bowl on the counter, eggs cracking, the whisk in the bowl, chopping. He started singing an Irish ballad. She could have sat there for hours listening to his rich, baritone voice. His influence pushed against her heart again. Had she ever been treated with such caring and kindness? She didn't think so. It soothed her soul and ignited a desire in her that she had no business feeling.

She frowned and stood. "Anything I can do to help?"

"No. I've got it."

"Then I'll feed Bitsy, Sawyer, and Chinchy. They haven't eaten anything since lunch."

Lainie stood and went to prepare the food for the critters. She was surprised that she hadn't seen Sawyer since returning from the winery. She found him upstairs sleeping under the peach-colored chair with Chinchy curled up between his paws. He must have been tired out from their excursion today, too. She left their food in the usual spot in the bathroom before returning to the kitchen.

"They're both asleep, I'd say we all felt the strain of today's adventure."

"Aye."

Lainie smiled to herself and had to refrain from telling him to return to his singing.

"Dinner is ready," he announced. "We'll eat on the porch."

"Sounds great."

"You go on out. I'll bring the food."

She didn't do exactly as he said. Instead, she walked through the kitchen, getting napkins and silverware.

"Hey. The porch."

"I'm only helping." She laughed.

He followed her out with two glasses of wine, placing them on the table. Then he pulled the chair out for her to sit. "Thank you," she said, taken aback.

"Nae problem. I'll be right back."

She'd barely had time to sip her wine before he set two plates on the table with perfect veggie omelets, a side of cantaloupe, and a croissant on them. With the Thanksgiving leftovers, she'd forgotten she had bought the croissants, a favorite.

"You're taking the cooking shows to heart. The omelets look amazing."

"Hope you like it. The secret's in adding a little cream and beating it thoroughly."

She nodded, slicing off a bite and eating it. "Mmm. This is fabulous."

"Thank you," Kalen said.

They ate in silence for several minutes, then Lainie asked, "Do you think I'll always have to fight off creatures over the magic of the timepiece?"

"Possibly. Not always with steel," he added. "Sometimes with choices. Sometimes with knowledge."

Lainie scraped the last bite of the omelet onto her fork and ate it, disappointed that she was finished and longing for one more taste. "I never dreamed I'd have something that someone else would covet, let alone kill for."

"You said your grandmother gave it to you?"

"Yes. I wonder how she managed to avoid the magic chasers. Maybe I'll ask my mom. I didn't know anything about the timepiece until Nana gave it to me when I turned thirteen. She'd said something about carrying on the McClure legacy. But again, no clue what that means."

"It sounds like she kept it secret."

"That's part of what I need to find out. I have the feeling she somehow tucked it away until she gave it to me. But then again, would you give your granddaughter something if you believed it could bring her harm? And there wasn't an indication of magic until I removed it from the box and wound it. So maybe the box protected it from other supernatural creatures, or maybe it was dormant until I wound it."

"Well, it's not dormant any longer," Kalen said.

"Duh. Nothing like stating the obvious." She sensed the timepiece was about more than magic. She grew thoughtful for a long moment. It was more than luck ruling her choices. It was about believing in miracles. It was about giving her a new life.

"What does 'duh' mean?"

She chuckled. "You say it when someone says something obvious, implying it was a stupid comment." Her laugh turned into a yawn. Even though she'd slept on the couch earlier, she was still tired.

"All right. Duh."

Lainie gave him an E for effort. "Today has been a crazy day. I'm tired and going to bed." She stood, gathering the dishes. Kalen helped by carrying the drink glasses.

She loaded the dishwasher and ran it. He washed the pan. There was an intimacy about the encounter that sparked a desire in Lainie that she hadn't felt for an exceptionally long time. The desire to be held. Not sexual, or needy, but a comforting exchange between two people growing closer. She blinked the thought away as she leaned against the counter. "Do you miss being in the book? Are you heartbroken to be taken away from Julia? She's your love interest, correct?"

He placed the clean pan onto the stovetop. "I don't miss Julia because in the book, I hadn't met her yet. It's sort of like time travel. I'm in two places at once, almost like there are two of me. While I'm here, I'm totally enjoying being here. I like learning and experiencing new things."

Lainie considered that. She likened it to taking a trip, and exploring new places. She'd had more opportunities to travel as a child than she'd had in her adult life with John. However, she always enjoyed coming home, too.

How would Kalen feel when he returned to the book? Would he be as nonchalant about Lainie and their time together as he was about Julia? Did Lainie mean anything to him? She felt like they were becoming friends. She enjoyed his company.

"I'm going to bed. See you in the morning. Goodnight."

"Goodnight."

Lainie fell asleep as soon as her head hit the pillow. She dreamed of flying through the air on the back of a beautiful dragon.

CHAPTER FOURTEEN

Comfort Before Style

On Saturday, Lainie woke at seven to the call of nature—she had been so tired she hadn't woken for her usual pee-run, or two, in the middle of the night. Shuffling back into the bedroom, she thought about the kids and what they might be doing today with their grandparents. Then, with nothing pressing that had to be done, she climbed back in bed, curling onto her side and snuggling beneath the covers. Overnight, it had grown chilly.

Black Friday spilled over into the weekend, with extended specials and sales to draw in shoppers. There wasn't anything Lainie wanted badly enough to fight the crowds. Instead, she lay there dreaming about the vineyard, the plans forming in her head. There would be a wine-tasting room, community functions, perhaps with live entertainment, and weddings. Happy occasions that would turn out better than hers had. There were tons of things she needed to learn, but the prospect excited her.

Around nine, she rose and dressed.

As she fixed her first cup of coffee, looking forward to the smooth taste of a new vanilla creamer she'd added, the doorbell rang. Lainie tightened her grip on the coffee cup. Kalen peeked out from his room to watch her open the front door. After wolfman's forced entry yesterday morning, he seemed more attentive and watchful.

Lainie set her cup of coffee on the counter and went to open the door. On the other side of the threshold stood a sheriff's officer. Her heart jumped in her chest. Why would an officer be at her residence? In rapid-fire, thoughts pulsed in her head. Were Jenna and Brennon okay? Her parents? Kalen? Had he done something stupid again like when he chased the goblin into the street while brandishing a sword? No, he was right here.

"Good morning. Are you Mrs. Cassidy?" he asked, seeming a bit uncomfortable.

She tensed. "Yes."

"Your husband is John Cassidy?"

"Yes."

"I'm sorry, ma'am, but your husband was taken to the hospital last night. The ER team was unable to revive him from his unconscious state, and he died shortly after midnight."

Lainie's knees almost buckled. She placed a hand on the doorframe to remain standing. "What? How?"

"The initial report is a drug overdose. Fentanyl. We were too late."

Lainie's eyes misted, her throat tightening. She covered her mouth with her hand to stifle a sob. So many thoughts and emotions raced through her mind. She couldn't live with John any longer, but she never wanted him dead. He was the father of her children. Oh God, the kids. How would she tell them? They hadn't had an easy life with their dad either, but they loved him. They would be crushed.

She sniffed and fought the tears. She wasn't normally a crier, but when she did, it was ugly. "How did you find him?"

"The woman with him called it in. I'm sorry for your loss. Please accept my condolences on his death," he said, his voice filled with compassion.

She nodded. "We're in the middle of a divorce."

Had John's drinking led to drugs? Had the woman introduced them to him? Had he been doing drugs while she was still with him? Even though she knew this wasn't her fault, she couldn't stop the guilt from setting in. If she'd still been with him, would he be dead? Could she have prevented this?

"The woman mentioned that. You will need to call the coroner's office to make arrangements and let them know your wishes," the officer said.

Again, she nodded, dazed. "Okay. Thank you." The officer turned away, and Lainie shut the door. She stood frozen in place. John was dead.

She took several deep breaths, but she couldn't stop the tears that followed. She'd wanted to be rid of him, but not like this. That soft part of her that always gave in to him, that always hoped they could make it work, that always loved the man she'd married even though that man had disappeared a long time ago—that soft part of her broke.

Kalen came out of his room with open arms. She stepped into them. He was the source of comfort that she needed, just for a moment. She pressed her face into the hollow of his shoulder and wept, more for the heartbreak it would cause her children than for herself.

Kalen didn't say anything. He simply held her until she'd spent the tears of shock, guilt, and grief.

She sniffed and stepped back. "I'm sorry. I got your shirt wet."

"I have another shirt."

She slowly walked back into the kitchen. Seeing her cup of coffee, she took a sip, looking for the comfort it often offered. The flavor didn't appeal to her the way it had earlier. Darn it, why did life have to be so hard? Just when something wonderful was on the brink of happening, life knocked her down.

"So now what?" Kalen asked, walking into the kitchen.

"It will be up to me to deal with John's funeral and tell the kids." She needed to keep her head on straight. "I...I just don't know where to begin. I've never had to deal with someone dying before."

Despite her uncertainty, she did a Google search, selected a funeral home, and called them, turning all the arrangements over to them.

The visit from the sheriff's deputy was the start of the longest week of her life. On Sunday, her parents brought the kids home as planned. Lainie asked her parents to stay and sat everyone down together to give them the horrible news. That way, there were more arms to hug and hold Jenna and Brennon in their grief.

Lainie called Karen to give her the news. "I'm so sorry for your loss," Karen said.

"Thank you. I expected a divorce not a funeral."

"I know. Do you think you still want to buy the vineyard?"

"Oh yes. I'm looking ahead, not back. The vineyard is my future," Lainie said.

"Got it. Just making sure."

"Yep. Continue as planned. Let me know the when and where, and I'll be there," Lainie said, watching her parents and kids fix lunch in the kitchen.

"Okay. I'll see you later. Hey, can I drop a casserole by this evening?"

Lainie hadn't thought about dinner. "Sure."

"What's this about a vineyard?" her mom asked when Lainie got off the phone.

"Well, it feels odd to share what I think is really good news on a day when we've received such tragic news, but..." She looked at her kids, knowing they were still reeling from the news about their dad and this was going to present a real change in their lives. "As you know, our rental is up here in two weeks. I've been looking for a new place for a week or so, and the other day, I found what I think will be perfect for us. It's a home with a vineyard."

Her dad's brows shot up. There was hesitation in his voice. "Wow, honey. That's great."

"We're not going back to the trailer?" Jenna asked.

"Do you want to live there?" Lainie asked.

"No," Brennon said.

Jenna reluctantly shook her head. "No. But there are some things there I'd like to get."

Lainie reached out to draw Jenna into her arms. "Me, too. We can do that later, after we're settled. Okay?"

"Yeah."

Sawyer walked by rubbing his side along Jenna's leg. She picked the cat up. "I think he's trying to make me feel better."

"You could be right," Lainie said.

At five-thirty, the doorbell rang. Anxiety trickled through Lainie as she reached for the doorknob, remembering what had greeted her the last few times she'd opened the door. She peered through the peephole. Karen and the entire bougie gang filled the porch.

Lainie swung the door wide. Her friends each held a covered dish. "Hi. Everyone wanted to help when I called. I hope that's okay," Karen said.

"Of course," Lainie replied, smiling and stepping back. "Come in."

Karen, Alaina, Shreena, Nandita, and Picku filed into the kitchen. They arranged the dishes on the island counter. Lainie called Jenna and Brennon from their bedrooms to meet the girls. They'd met Karen and Alaina, but not the others.

Lainie quickly introduced everyone, then added, "Thank you for the meal. You went above and beyond."

"That's what friends are for," Alaina added.

"If you or the kids need to talk, my door is always open," Picku said. "Don't rush your grief. It's a natural process."

Ah, Picku the therapist, Lainie thought. But Jenna and Brennon may need some counseling. "Thank you," Lainie said. "I'll keep that in mind. I think we're all still in shock, right now."

"We were supposed to spend next weekend with Dad," Jenna said, her tone laced with bitterness as her eyes bore into Lainie.

Jenna needed someone to blame for this. Right now, her mother was it. Lainie's feelings were all over the place. The kids were probably experiencing similar feelings.

If John had been using drugs and had a girlfriend living at the house, Lainie certainly wouldn't have wanted the kids over there to see evidence of that. Knowing he'd died of a drug overdose was bad enough, and she had to watch herself that she wasn't casting aspersions about the choices he'd made since they'd left him. Since she'd left him.

Lainie watched Alaina and Kalen laugh about something. She hoped they didn't say anything in front of the kids about Friday's portal trip. She still planned to keep the timepiece a secret.

Thankfully, the gals wrapped up their visit. "Let us know about the arrangements," Karen said before leaving.

On Monday, the kids went to school as usual. Lainie thought it best to keep them busy. If they stayed home, all they would do was mope around the house.

Lainie called her lawyer to make her aware of John's passing. Nicole informed her that the court would dismiss the case since the divorce wasn't yet final—you couldn't divorce someone who was deceased. That meant everything of his was now hers. Not that she wanted any of it, except for the pictures of when the kids were young. Those were in the trailer. She grew thoughtful. She had been afraid she'd never get those back.

When she'd called Becky, the owner of the dance studio, to tell her about John, she'd insisted Lainie didn't have to teach classes that week. Lainie had figured she'd say that but didn't want to skip classes. They were her joy. Plus, it was good to keep the kids in their regular routine.

Tuesday, Lainie had an appointment with the funeral home. She finalized all the details and paid the bill. There would be a ton of things that would require her attention moving forward, but all of them could be put off for a while.

As she pulled into the driveway, she saw Sarah from the pawn shop and Wolfie together across the street, watching the house. If the two had paired up, that could only mean trouble. The notion frightened her. When she got inside, she pointed them out to Kalen. He wanted to march after them, sword in hand, but she touched his arm, stopping him. "We'll deal with them when we must."

"They sense a vulnerability in you now. A weakness. That's why they're here. They're like predators ready to pounce on a wounded animal."

"But I have you. So, we'll wait and watch."

He scowled but nodded.

"No," she said, surprising herself with how steady her voice sounded. "Charging now gives them what they want — reaction, chaos, exposure. We wait, assess, and choose ground that favors us."

His scowl shifted, approval flickering in his eyes. She was learning — not just to fight, but to *think*.

Wednesday, Karen called with an update on the purchase of the vineyard. Everything was set. They could finalize the transaction on Saturday if she was up to it. Lainie wanted to move forward with the property. The clock was ticking. She only had a week and half left on her rental. If she closed the deal on Saturday, perhaps they could start moving in on Sunday. That would give them a week's leeway. And if the deal fell through, well, she'd have to find somewhere else to live.

One thing she knew for certain; there was no way they would live in John's trailer again, even though it was technically hers now. Too much hurt came with the place.

Thursday, Lainie cleaned the house and did laundry. It was what she did whenever she needed to keep busy. Sawyer seemed to follow her around. Ever since the portal episode, she couldn't think of Sawyer as just a cat any longer. He'd changed into a knight. *Maybe she should call him Sir Sawyer now*, she joked to herself.

On Friday, they had a celebration of life. It was nice. *Better than what he deserved*, a small voice in her head whispered. Most of the people who attended were John's coworkers and a few church members. Once again, Lainie spotted Sarah and Wolfie off in the distance, watching. It gave her the creeps. It was like watching a storm brewing. *You knew it was going to hit, you just didn't know how bad it would be. Might be a long, slow soaker. Might throw off a tornado.*

And then it was over. Lainie said goodbye to everyone as they left. Her friends stayed to help her clean up. Brennon seemed to take everything in stride, but Jenna took it hard. Lainie knew it would take time and healing to move into their new stage of life.

She anticipated good days and bad days. But she would get through them, just like she always had. So far, she'd survived one hundred percent of her worst days. She would tomorrow, too. She was determined to live her best life now.

CHAPTER FIFTEEN

Ehh. I've Gained Thirty Pounds
Overnight

Lᴀɪɴɪᴇ sᴘᴇɴᴛ ᴇᴀʀʟʏ Sᴀᴛᴜʀᴅᴀʏ morning counting the money and packing two duffle bags. It had been thirty-one days since the first magical money had appeared. That totaled one million five hundred and fifty thousand dollars. Her pulse raced as she handled it. *Un-freaking-believable.* She'd spent some of it, but that had been a drop in the bucket. Now, she packed one million to pay for the property. The transaction would take place at Karen's office.

She drove her van to the office, arriving early. Noting the sign, she hadn't realized that Karen was a Real Estate Broker. Lainie wasn't sure how that differed from an agent. Maybe it meant Karen owned the business.

After glancing around the parking lot, she carried the bags inside. Taking the timepiece with her was second-nature now, but she took extra care to have it this week. She needed all the good luck and magic she could get.

Lainie cherished the consistent things in her life that the timepiece had given her. The magic money was deposited in her purse each morning. And some kind of dessert materialized every day. She didn't want to think about how many calories she consumed. She'd worry about that later.

Even though she knew how the money came to her, she couldn't help feeling the tiniest bit of guilt over having it. Plus, she worried if someone saw it, they'd think she'd done something illegal. People she knew didn't have duffle bags stuffed with money.

When Charlie arrived, he walked over to her with a warm, gentle expression. "I'm sorry about your husband passing."

"Ex-husband. But thank you. It's been difficult for the kids."

"I imagine so. When my Sue died, I didn't want to go on. Then I realized I wanted to live for her."

Lainie's throat tightened. What would it be like to have that kind of love? She'd probably never know. She gave herself a shake and put it out of her mind. *Press onward to a new day.*

The transaction went smoothly. Karen had all the paperwork in order. Lainie read the promissory note, signed it, and handed over the funds. When Charlie gave her the keys, she closed her fingers around them, bringing them against her chest. This was more than she'd dreamed of.

"I've already moved into the guest house as we've agreed. My niece's wedding will be on December eighteenth. We've established that it will go on as planned. Right?"

"Yes. I'm excited about the wedding." But having only two weeks to prepare could be difficult to pull off. Although, all she had to do was work with the wedding planners, which should be easy enough.

"I'm looking forward to introducing you to the staff and helping you get the hang of the winery."

"As am I. Thank you," Lainie said.

"When do think you'll start moving in?" Lambert asked.

"Probably tomorrow. We don't have much. Just what I could pack in my van when we left our home. I only have the rental house until the end of next week."

Charlie's face softened. "It sounds like you've been through a lot lately."

She shrugged. "That's life. I'm super excited about this move, though. Thanks for working with me to make this happen. Someday, you'll have to tell me about your dream."

His eyes narrowed for a second as if he were processing what she'd said. "Oh, yeah. One of these days. Maybe when we're sitting on the porch sipping wine."

Karen had been busy making copies of the papers. She rejoined them. "Okay, we're finished." She handed them each a packet of the paperwork, then walked them to the door.

"I'll probably see you tomorrow," Lainie said to Charlie.

"Call me if you need anything, or when you're ready for a more intensive tour of the winery. You have my number."

"Great. I'll give you a call."

He gave her a wave and let himself out.

"And let me know if you need help moving," Karen said.

"Okay. Will do." Lainie didn't anticipate needing help, though. It could most likely be accomplished in a couple of trips, especially with Kalen's help.

Lainie felt bad about feeling so good the day after her ex-husband's memorial. As she drove home, she turned on the radio and sang along. Her euphoria lasted until she parked the van in the driveway. When she walked into the house, it was about the kids.

The clank of the foosball table from above told her Brennon was upstairs. She'd bet she'd find Jenna in her bedroom. Bitsy ran over and begged, pumping her paws up and down, demanding to be picked up. Lainie obliged. "Have you been a good girl this morning?"

Lainie stroked her neck before setting her down. "So, let's see what's happening."

Kalen strolled in from the porch, Chinchy on his shoulder. "Did it go well?"

"Yep. I'm a home and business owner. We'll begin moving tomorrow."

He nodded. "Good."

Lainie lowered her voice. "I'm worried that Jenna and Brennon won't be thrilled, though."

"Are you happy with it?"

She couldn't help her smile. "Oh yes. It's perfect."

"Then you'll make it work. I've watched you. You're good with your children. You're an awesome mother."

"Well, look at you. I can't believe you just used the word awesome." Lainie chuckled.

"TV is an excellent teacher."

"I don't know about that," she said, heading to the kitchen to get a drink to take upstairs. She took a coke from the fridge, then popped the top. Her stomach tightened with every step up the stairs. She dipped her head in the game room. "How's it going?" she asked Brennon.

"Fine."

"Who's winning?"

He raised his brows, then he realized she was teasing. She laughed. "Join me in Jenna's room for a minute so I can talk to you both."

She could have called them both downstairs, but the less she disturbed her daughter, the better the attitude she'd get. At least, that was the plan.

Lainie knocked on Jenna's door.

"Come in." Jenna lounged on her bed with headphones on. Listening to music, Lainie guessed. Sawyer stretched out at her feet.

Lainie would have to ask the cat about that later. She walked in, then sat on the edge of her daughter's bed the way she'd done thousands of times. "You doing okay?"

Jenna looked unsure. "I guess."

"It will take time."

"What's up?" Jenna asked, ignoring Lainie's statement.

"Well, we only have this rental through next week. And as you know, I've been actively looking for a permanent house for us." She paused, looking from Brennon to Jenna for any initial feedback, but got none. "Well, I found a place that I think you'll really like, and... Well, I closed on it this morning. We can start moving tomorrow." Lainie didn't want to oversell the place. Sometimes, as soon as the kids picked up on how much she liked something, they gravitated toward the opposite stance.

Jenna pushed up in the bed. "Bye-bye swimming pool," she grumbled.

"Actually, it has a pool."

"Awesome," Brennon said.

"It comes furnished. We can change the furnishings over time. You can do whatever you want with your bedrooms."

Jenna shrugged. "Whatever."

Lainie looked at Brennon. "We'll load up both vans tomorrow to begin taking stuff over there."

"Is Kalen coming, too?" he asked.

The question caught Lainie off-guard. What was Brennon thinking? "Yes. He'll continue renting a room there."

Brennon looked dubious, but he didn't argue or say anything.

Lainie gave Jenna a kiss. "I love you. I'm sorry you're going through this hard time. I know it hurts."

"Love you, too," Jenna mumbled.

"If you guys pack your things this afternoon, they can be part of the first trip we take over there tomorrow, okay?" She stood, walking over to Brennon. She kissed him as well and wrapped both arms around him in a bear hug.

He hugged her back. "Thanks for looking out for us, Mom."

"Always." They both were good kids, and she was proud of them.

Brennon turned toward his room. Lainie went back downstairs, and Sawyer followed her. She told Kalen the same thing about packing.

"That will take me all of ten minutes."

"You're probably right." Lainie smiled. "But it still needs to be done. I want to leave in the morning."

The vans were loaded, ready to pull out. "I'm going to miss this house," Brennon said.

"Yeah. Even the color grew on me," Jenna added.

"I think you'll like the new house," Lainie said. "It's also a two-story with a pool." Those were the features she felt most interested the kids.

The one problem with the new house was its location. It meant a drive to their schools and to the dance studio. But with the vineyard, Lainie was willing to make those concessions. Plus, she hoped Jenna would agree to transfer to a closer school next year. She would press those issues later.

There were enough problems to deal with for now.

Sunday morning, Jenna, Bitsy, and Sawyer piled into the van with Lainie. Kalen and Chinchy rode with Brennon. They stopped for donuts, coffee, and drinks on the way.

"How far is this place?" Jenna asked with one of those put-upon, side-eye looks.

"We're almost there."

"I can't believe you bought something on the other side of town," Jenna said. "It's going to take forever to get to school."

"We'll work that out."

"I am *not* changing schools, Mom."

Lainie turned into the drive.

Jenna gasped, saying with distain, "Oh jeez. We're back out in the country again."

"It's not the same. Wait until you see the house." Lainie parked the van in front of the garage. She opened the rear hatch and removed a bottle of champagne, taking it with her. "We'll come back out for our stuff. Just get Bitsy and Sawyer."

Brennon pulled up beside her and cut the engine, hopping out of his van. "Mom, this is amazing. But really, what bank did you rob?"

Lainie chuckled. "I got a really good deal."

"You'd have to."

Kalen hung back, looking around. Lainie suspected he checked to see if their watchers had followed them.

Lainie paused on the porch, waiting until everyone gathered there. She held the keys in one hand and the bottle of champagne in the other. Inhaling a deep breath, she smashed the bottle on the porch railing. "Here's to new beginnings. I christen this house with love and good luck."

Brennon and Jenna stood with their mouths open. They were probably shocked that their mother had just made a mess that she'd have to clean up.

Lainie unlocked the door, then swung it open. "Go have a look."

Jenna and Brennon were like kids on Christmas morning. Lainie let them romp through the house, discovering the place for themselves. She set Bitsy inside. Sawyer strolled in on his own, finding a comfy chair near a window. Kalen let Chinchy roam at will.

Kalen had already seen the place along, with Alaina and Karen. He made his way into the kitchen where a basket sat on the counter. "Looks like someone left you a gift."

Lainie turned. She'd been looking in the pantry closet for a broom and dustpan to sweep up the glass on the porch. "Oh, how sweet. I'll be back in a moment to have a look."

After tossing the broken bottle and glass into the garbage, Lainie examined the basket. "There's a card." She pulled it loose, then read the note. "It's from the bougie bitches. Welcoming us to our new home." Lainie's heart melted. Her friends were the best.

Jenna and Brennon finally made their way into the kitchen. "The place is huge," Brennon said.

"Have you chosen your rooms? Like I said, we can paint and redecorate them however you want."

"Can I paint mine lavender?" Jenna asked.

"Sure."

Jenn's face lit up for the first time in a week. "Awesome."

"Let's unload the vans," Lainie said. They all went outside, then started carrying their things into the house. The kids unloaded their belongings first. Lainie directed Kalen to put the groceries in the kitchen. She'd put them away after everything was unpacked.

On her second trip, Lainie noticed three tall shadows standing near the entrance to the property. The hairs at the nape of her neck bristled. She squinted. Not for the first time, she thought it may be time for an eye appointment. She couldn't say for sure who the figures were, but she'd bet money that two of them were Sarah and Wolfie. Who was the third?

Kalen came out for another load. Lainie pointed out the stalkers. "We have company already. Only now, it's a trio."

"I wonder who joined them," Kalen commented. He stared. "I'm going to find out." Without warning, he ran forward, shedding his clothes, and transformed into his dragon form. Lainie gasped. He flew toward the trio. She was so stunned by his magnificent beauty that she forgot about the kids.

CHAPTER SIXTEEN

Everything Is a Chore

KALEN DID A LOW pass, banked, and then went for a second pass, flying low. He blew fire at the trespassers. They moved into a stand of trees where he couldn't get to them without landing.

Thank heavens this was acreage property and not rows of homes like in the rental's subdivision. Lainie wanted to yell at him to stop. Although, if she did that, it might attract more attention from the house than a dragon flying in the distance. At least where the kids were concerned.

She quickly took the final load into the house.

Brennon peered over the upstairs railing. "Anything else left in the van?" he asked.

"No. I think we have it all," Lainie responded. She told him there was no need to go back out.

"Let me know if you need anything else," Brennon said.

Can you talk down an irate dragon? Lainie thought. "Okay," she answered. She went back outside and stood, arms crossed, watching and waiting for Kalen to return. To her horror, she saw an arrow, then another fly toward Kalen. He did an evasive maneuver, rolling into a spiral. If it weren't been a dangerous situation, the acrobatics would have been beautiful to watch. Her heart hammered in her chest. She feared for his safety.

He dropped to the ground and pursued the three on foot, spewing fire to clear his path. Lainie worried the trees would ignite. She held her breath. She didn't want to have the fire department here on her first day. As Kalen spit another ball of fire, the trio vanished.

At the same time, from the direction of the guest house, a creature ran toward Kalen with incredible speed. He ate up the ground in seconds. Kalen transformed into his human body.

Lainie feared for Kalen's safety. He was far more vulnerable now. Why had he transformed into his weaker human form? The two seemed to exchange words. The creature removed his outer garment and handed it to Kalen, who wrapped it around his hips. Then it shifted into... Charles Lambert.

What was going on?

The two men turned and walked casually in Lainie's direction as if confronting supernatural beings was an everyday thing. The witch, werewolf, and whatever the third being was had disappeared, Charlie veered off toward the guest cottage.

As Kalen drew closer, Lainie noticed he had blood running down his arm from his bicep. "You're hurt."

"Just a scratch. An arrow nicked me."

"Which one shot the arrows at you?"

"The newcomer to the group. I think she's a nymph."

When he got to where his clothes were, he began to dress.

"Leave your shirt off."

He peered over his shoulder at her, raising a saucy brow.

She huffed. "You'll get blood all over it. Your wound should be washed and bandaged first."

"And here I thought you were admiring my physique. You know, like the ladies do in the romance novels." He shot her a wicked smile.

She turned her back to him as heat rushed into her face. He was too bold. And too close to the mark. She had been ogling him. How could she not when he'd stripped to change into his dragon form and then again when he'd dressed right in front of her?

Lainie led the way inside and then to the kitchen sink where she found some paper towels and soap. She cleansed and dried the L-shaped wound. "This could probably use stitches."

"No. Shifters heal quickly. Just cover it with a bandage," he said.

She searched through cabinets until she found a first-aid kit. After he dressed, he turned to face her. "Mr. Lambert—Charlie—is a berserker. He'll be a great asset to add to the team."

Team? She didn't know she had a team. She pondered that. Well, maybe that was exactly what she needed. Kalen, Sawyer, Chinchy, Felicity, and now Charlie. They all seemed ready to protect her and the timepiece.

"What is a berserker?" Lainie had done some computer research into magic and magical things like the timepiece, but she hadn't come across any mention of a berserker.

"He's a fierce Norse warrior whose body changes from human into a seething ball of destructive energy. He's a thread away from losing control and turning into a killing machine."

"Oh my. Charlie doesn't seem like that type at all."

"Most of them work hard to keep that side of themselves under control. They are loners. Once they attach themselves to someone, they're extremely loyal. He seems to have made some connection with you."

"He'd said he knew I was to buy the vineyard," Lainie said.

"Perhaps he has more than berserker in him," Kalen suggested. "That would explain his self-control back there."

"I guess we'll have to wait and see." Although sometimes, she wasn't very patient. "What about the new creature in the trio? You think she's a nymph?"

"Yes, I overheard them talking as I flew over them. As we learned during our visit to Esidarap, the wood nymphs and fairies are at war. The nymphs are withholding lands where the fairies want to plant more flowers. The nymphs refuse to give up an ounce of forest. They see you as connected in some way to Felicity."

"She's the fairy of my timepiece. You know that." She paced a few steps and turned back. "I have nothing to do with that dimension."

"Because of your timepiece, they think you do."

"So, the very thing that is making my life better could be putting me in danger. I've known that ever since Sarah first tried to steal the talisman." She paused, thinking. "Okay, then. Now's when you get to earn your keep. We need a vigilant watch on the grounds. That makes you head of security."

He nodded.

"There are golf carts if you need them to patrol the place. You shouldn't fly in your dragon form except maybe at night," she said. "Even though it's a lot of property, a dragon is kinda hard to miss."

"Agreed. I'll try not to shapeshift. Except in the case of an emergency."

"Let's hope we don't have any of those." She gave herself a shake, thinking of the kids. She would keep them safe at all costs. Then her mind turned to all the things she had to do. She pulled up her to-do list on her phone to create a new file. "We're going to be busy for the next couple of weeks. I need to decorate for the holidays. Maybe my friends will help me. Our first vineyard wedding is Charlie's niece in just two weeks. He said the wedding planner will do all the work, but still, I want the place to be amazing."

"Just let me know what you need, and I'll do my best to help," he said.

"I'm going to need a lot of luck and a little bit of magic," she said. And for Sarah and her friends to stay away.

They weren't doing anything but trespassing. Hanging around, watching, plotting. She didn't know what they were up to; she just knew they were up to no good. And it wasn't as if she could call the police and report them.

Who were the supernatural police?

The first rays of the setting sun filtered through the back porch and across the pool, washing it in an orange glow. It was later than she'd thought.

Lainie looked up the nearest pizza restaurant on her phone and ordered delivery. As she did so, she noticed Kalen pouring two glasses of wine. "Pizza will arrive in forty-five minutes." *Not as quick as at the rental.*

He handed her a wine glass, then held his up for a toast. "Cheers."

She touched her glass to his. "Thanks. Let's sit on the porch."

She led the way, unlocking and opening the French doors. As she slid into the patio chair, she let go of the pent-up energy she'd been holding in throughout the week. John's memorial, the closing on the house, moving in...it had been one thing after another.

Lainie sipped her wine, relaxing and watching the day fade away. A few stars became visible. "I used to wish upon the first star that came out at night. We were taught to keep wishes secret when we blew out our birthday candles or saw a shooting star. If you told someone the wish, it wouldn't come true. They had that wrong. Wishes are the most powerful when you tell someone or say them aloud."

"What do you wish for now?" Kalen asked.

"I haven't decided yet."

The air grew chilly as the sky darkened. The pool area didn't have a screened enclosure. She liked sitting outdoors like this. It wasn't something she'd ever been able to do at the trailer. That time seemed far away now.

The doorbell rang. She jumped up, took cash from her wallet, and gave the delivery guy a generous tip. When she came back into the kitchen, both Jenna and Brennon looked down at her from the walking bridge that cut across upstairs. "Pizza," she announced.

"I think pizza is becoming our family meal," Brennon said. "Not that I'm complaining, mind you."

Lainie had grown lax in the cooking department. Maybe she should even try conjuring up some meals that didn't involve chocolate. Naw. Best to reserve magic for important things like dessert.

After dinner, the kids disappeared into their rooms again. "I'm going to take a shower," Kalen announced.

"That's probably a good idea. You get all hot and sweaty in your dragon form, right?"

He grinned. "Yes. I suppose so." He rose, then cleaned up the kitchen before heading off, crushing and throwing the pizza box in the trash.

As he walked into his room, Lainie found her computer case among a stack of things that still needed to be put away. She carried it into the family room. She turned on the TV for some background noise, then got to work searching for Christmas decorations online. Maybe she'd see if the girls would be available next weekend to help her decorate.

She sent a group text asking them to join her on Saturday for a wine-tasting and decorating party. But this place was so big, it may be too much to decorate the whole place. Then she thought about sending a shout-out to her niece. Alexa owned an up-and-coming interior-decorating business. She'd even secured a weekly local television spotlight. Perhaps she could connect Lainie with a crew to decorate.

Lainie bit her lip, looking at several pictures on Pinterest. Maybe she could use magic to get the job done. It would give her extra incentive to practice using magic. She smiled. A flutter of excitement beat in her tummy.

CHAPTER SEVENTEEN

Don't Annoy Me

LAINIE BEGAN HER DAY with a walk at sunrise. Perhaps it would become a new tradition. The morning air smelled fresh and green as she walked the grounds of the vineyard. Not the entire vineyard. There wasn't enough time for that. She strolled past the cottage and barn and along the closest plot of vines. The dew hung on the grass. Her sneakers were wet by the time she returned to the house, where she fixed a cup of coffee and added more tasks to her to-do list, including meeting with the wedding planner.

They were in a brand-new place, but it was the same routine. Basically. Brennon drove himself to school, only now, it was twice as far and took much longer to get there. Lainie had to take Jenna to school in the mornings, except on Mondays, dance day. Lainie would pick up Jenna after school, and they'd eat takeout, then go to the dance studio. The rest of the week, Brennon would hang around after school to bring his sister home.

Tonight, as she walked to her van after classes, she had a sudden flashback to the time John had confronted them in the parking lot. The timepiece had come to her rescue and pushed him back. That had been a couple of months ago.

"What's wrong?" Jenna asked.

"Nothing," she said, trying to school her expression. She knew those memories would fade, but not quickly enough.

They got into the van, and she began the drive home. "What made you buy that place, Mom?" Jenna asked. "It's so far away."

"I don't know. I felt it in my gut that it was meant to be ours. The vineyard is a source of revenue, and we'll have additional income with it being a great venue for weddings."

"A wedding venue? Cool. You didn't say anything about that." Jenna lowered her phone to glance at her mom.

"There's been a lot going on." She turned onto the freeway. "The first wedding is the weekend after next. It's Mr. Lambert's niece."

"So do we attend all these weddings?"

"I don't think so. We're providing the venue. That's all. I'm sure we'll figure it out as we go along."

"I don't want to change schools," Jenna said unexpectedly.

"We're not going to deal with that this year. I'll drive you. Brennon will pick you up. Things will stay the same for now."

"Until May?" Jenna asked with a snicker.

"Yes. And then we'll see about next year. You'll be going into high school then and changing schools anyway." Lainie grimaced, glad it was dark so Jenna couldn't see her face. She wasn't as upset about the school issue as she was about her baby girl growing up.

The following morning, Lainie met with the wedding planner. Her name was Marianne. She was tall, with curly, shoulder-length brown hair.

"Tell me your plans," Lainie said.

"It will be a small wedding, with about eighty people attending. The ceremony will take place overlooking the lake. There will be seating for the guests, fifty chairs on each side of the center aisle, allowing for extra overflow." Marianne was a bundle of energy who talked fast. Lainie liked her.

"The guest house will be used for the bridal party, dressing and getting ready prior to the wedding."

"Mr. Lambert is on board with that?" Lainie asked. They walked past the cottage toward the barn.

"Yes. It's all arranged. The guests will transition to a dining area off of the barn, beneath the covered carport. We'll have twelve round tables. A DJ will be set up over there." She pointed toward the edge of the vineyard. "Dinner will be served buffet style and managed from inside the barn."

"What about parking and restrooms?"

"Parking will be in the west field on the other side of the guest house. There are restrooms in the barn."

"Excellent. Is there anything I can do? I'm putting up Christmas decorations this week at the entrance and around my house." Her house. That was actually real.

"No. I told Mr. Lambert and his niece, Annabelle, we would handle the entire event."

"Okay. Great. Perhaps this will be the first of many," Lainie suggested.

Marianne smiled. "That would be awesome."

As Marianne drove away, Charlie came out of the barn and caught up with Lainie. She hadn't spoken to him since the incident last night.

"Marianne is nice," she said.

"Yes. Sue had found her and made the original arrangements before she passed. It gave her such pleasure to be able to contribute to the wedding."

Lainie nodded slowly. "So, you're a berserker."

"Mixed breed. My father is berserker. Mom a sorcerer. They live in Norway." He crossed his arms over his big chest. "It's the reason I knew you'd buy this place. I saw it in a dream, but I also sensed the magic in you."

"Hmm." She believed he was wrong about the last. The talisman conveyed the power.

"How long have they been watching you?"

"A few weeks now. It looks like the witch has been recruiting," Lainie said, exasperated. "I'm worried about what comes after the watching."

Charlie hesitated then, his expression shifting in a way that made Lainie straighten.

"And there's someone else," he added softly. "Not part of the witch's circles. Older. More dangerous. They call him the Collector." He glanced toward the bare vines, as if expecting to see someone among the shadows. "If he's sniffing around, it's not you he's after—it's whatever you're carrying that he wants." His gaze dropped pointedly to her purse.

A chill rippled down her spine, subtle but certain, as though the very mention of the Collector caused the air to recoil.

"I'll keep my eyes open," Charlie said. "Don't hesitate to give me a shout if you need anything."

"Thank you. I appreciate that."

"If you stop by Wednesday morning—Wednesdays are half-days—or anytime Thursday, I'll introduce you to the vineyard staff." He paused, glancing back at the barn, then at her again.

"Okay. I'll drop by. Thanks." As she walked back to the house, Lainie felt a little safer knowing Charlie could handle himself and had magical powers. If only she knew what she was doing and had full control of the timepiece's magic, she'd feel a whole lot better.

In the house, after lunch, she took out the timepiece and opened her laptop.

Kalen looked on. "What are you doing?"

"So far, everything I've conjured has come from pictures, predominantly of recipes from the dessert magazine, except for what the talisman has decided to give me. Now, I'm going to try to conjure Christmas decorations from the computer images."

"Getting brave."

"I should give this more attention. I'll never learn how it works if I don't practice it." She stood, opened the cover of the watch, and held the timepiece out at arm's length. Holding the image on the screen in her mind's eye, she concentrated on making it appear.

The magic flowed through her hand, curling forth and across the space in the room. It reminded her of the wind. She couldn't see it, but she could feel it dance across her skin and see the results it produced when the tree branches bent. Two miniature nutcracker cookies appeared on the counter.

"What?" She lifted them. That wasn't what she was going for. Her gaze flicked to Kalen. "Cookies? I got cookies. The timepiece must want me to be some fat-assed bougie bitch. It's always giving me sweets."

"You like sweets," Kalen said, laughing.

"Not funny."

Just as she grinned at the tiny nutcracker perched proudly on her palm, the timepiece gave a soft, rhythmic thrum—like a distant heartbeat only tapping against metal. Not hers. Not the magic she'd just cast. Something external. She angled her chin to the side, trying to find the sound. Her smile slipped.

It wasn't just her pushing magic outward anymore — something was pushing back. Maybe controlling power wasn't only force, but defense against influence.

Kalen lifted his head sharply, nostrils flaring as if he scented something unfamiliar. "Did you feel that?" he muttered.

Lainie swallowed, suddenly aware of how still the air had become, how the shadows in the corners seemed to gather forward. She told herself it was nothing... even as the timepiece settled again with the quiet finality of a held breath.

"Yeah." She shook her head. "It wasn't me. Sort of felt like an intrusion."

They waited, looking at each other in silence.

Kalen shrugged. "Humph. Try again."

She did. Seven more times. Every time, she got cookies. She growled low in her throat.

"What's different?" he asked.

"I'm trying to project from the computer. Maybe I need to imagine it differently. Life-sized."

"Try it."

She did. Two life-sized nutcrackers materialized in the open space across the room.

Lainie released the breath she'd been holding. "It worked." She smiled.

"Excellent," Kalen said.

"Thank you," she said, modestly. "Please carry them to the front porch and place one on each side of the door."

As he did, Lainie carried the computer with her and moved to the second item on her Pinterest page. This time, she conjured garland on the banister. Again, the magic worked, making cookies first. After several attempts, she finally got the garland she was trying to get. It was both exhilarating and terrifying. She could sense the power circling through her and out of the timepiece.

Kalen returned as she was adding a half-dozen garland pieces to the cookie tray.

He picked one up and ate it. "You've got cookies down pat."

"Ya think?"

Next, she created a Christmas tree in the living room, decked out in a bird theme with teal, gold, and white ornaments. She moved from room to room, repeating the process of imagining the pictured item where she wanted it. There were white candles and gold reindeer on the mantle and wreaths in every window on the front of the house.

An hour later, she circled back to the kitchen counter, feeling quite drained. Perhaps she'd gotten carried away and done too much. She wanted to involve the kids in the selection and decoration of the tree that would go in the family room.

She closed the laptop. "That's it for today," she told Kalen. "This is a lot easier than shopping for everything and doing it by hand."

"Do you think you went a little overboard?" Kalen asked.

"Well, it's more than I've ever done in the past. But then again, I didn't have this kind of space, or money, or magic." She'd need to go by the trailer and retrieve their traditional Christmas ornaments and decorations. She wasn't looking forward to doing that. Should she take the kids, or do it when they were in school? That was something else to decide. "Want a drink?" she asked Kalen as she strolled to the fridge.

"Please."

She removed a coke for herself and fruit-punch-flavored Gatorade for him. He still wasn't fond of carbonated drinks. She handed him the drink. "Let's take a ride out to the entrance. I'd like to get a better idea for outside decorations. I'll start on those tomorrow."

Lainie opened the garage. "Here." She held out the key to the golf cart. "You drive."

He stared at her, then nodded, accepting the key.

"We're on private property. You don't need a license to drive here. Not like cars on the highway. When you feel comfortable with it, you can drive it over to the winery."

"Okay." He slid onto the bench on the driver's side. She took the passenger's side, chewing on her lower lip. How hard could it be? Even Jenna could drive a golf cart.

They both reached for seat belts, but found none. Apparently, they weren't a standard feature on golf carts. Thankfully, Charlie had parked the carts facing out, so Kalen didn't need to back up right away.

Since he hadn't driven any sort of motor vehicle before, she thought it wise to give him instructions. "At your feet, there are two pedals. The left is the brake, the right is the accelerator. First, place your right foot on the brake and hold it there until you're ready to go."

It seemed to take a moment for him to process which was his right foot. She wondered if they identified that in his time period.

"Okay. Insert the key in the ignition. See that it has three positions: an F for forward, R for reverse, and OFF. So we want to go forward, so turn it to the F." He followed her instructions. So far, so good.

"Now, with your foot on the brake, we will stay at a stop. When you're ready, move your right foot over to the accelerator, and gently press down. As he did, the cart rolled slowly forward. "To go faster, just push down more, but gently."

Kalen pushed a little too hard, and the cart lurched forward. "Gently," she yelled.

He removed his foot. They slowed abruptly.

"Easy. Easy. Push down slowly, let off slowly."

He tried. The cart did several jerky starts and stops. Gradually, the forward motion grew longer and less jerky.

"Okay, so with the steering wheel, you need to turn it left or right, but again, slowly, or we will tip over." He did a few practice turns left and right, then straightened out. "Good. We're heading out to the front gate," she said with a wave of her hand.

"Right." He altered his steering to aim in that direction. She leaned slightly out the side, steading herself with a hand. She was missing the seat belts right about now.

They stopped at the gate. She got out and looked back at the house and winery from the street, envisioning what decorations might look good. Perhaps she'd line the entry with lighted Christmas trees. The wedding would be at sunset with a dinner to follow. An array of white lights would give it a magical feel.

She hopped back into the cart. "Okay. I have some ideas. I'll work on this tomorrow after the winery staff has gone for the day. I wouldn't want an audience for my magic."

"Of course not."

"This time you'll want to go in reverse," she instructed. "So turn the key to the R."

He put it in reverse and tapped the gas pedal. They zoomed backward.

"Whoa," she said, grabbing the dash.

"Easy?" he said, raising a brow.

"Yeah. It needs a gentle touch." She brushed tendrils of hair from her eyes. "Now, we want to go forward. So what do you do?"

He turned the key to the "F" position and turned to her with a smile.

"Good," she said. He drove them back to the house with only a few jerks along the way. He was getting the hang of it.

"You can pull it straight in," she said about parking it in the garage.

"No. It was backed in when I got it. I'll do the same."

She pressed her lips together. "If that's what you're set on doing."

Evidently, he was. He pulled around, put the cart in reverse and, with short spurts of motion, navigated the cart safely into the parking spot. Pretty as you please. He shot her a look of satisfaction as he turned off the cart and removed the key.

"Good job. Now, press hard on the brake until you feel it click," she said. "That sets the emergency brake and prevents the cart from rolling."

"That was fun." Lainie got out of the cart, feeling exhilarated. She'd taught him something new. Did that count as an exchange for him teaching her how to wield a sword? "Now that you're familiar with how it operates, you're welcome to take the cart whenever you need to see Charlie or the vineyard."

As she walked around the cart to the door into the house, he took hold of her wrist and spun her to face him. Her body moved closer, almost touching his broad chest. She inhaled a quick breath. Flecks of gold danced in his eyes.

"Thank you," he said.

His voice rumbled over her. She shivered from nerves rather than cold. "For what?"

"For trusting me."

Lainie cocked her head and gently slid her wrist out of his grasp. He let her go but held her gaze. "If you're going to live in this world, then you need to learn to be part of it."

"I'm ready."

She nodded. Perhaps he was. She knew though, he could be sent back into his book world at any time. *Don't get attached to him*, she told herself.

She gave herself a shake. I may be too late for that.

CHAPTER EIGHTEEN

Where's My Favorite Spatula?

WEDNESDAY AFTERNOON KAREN CAME over. The winery staff had the day off, so Lainie didn't have to worry about them seeing her doing magic. This was a chance for her to have some fun with the magic as Karen had suggested. She handed Karen a cookie tin to carry.

"What's this for?" Karen asked. "It's empty."

"Not for long. It seems I'm the cookie whisper. Whatever I'm trying to create comes to me in the form of a cookie first. Crazy, I know."

Karen shrugged.

"We'll take the cart and start at the road first, then work our way up to the house," Lainie said. They both hopped in the golf cart, and she drove down the drive. Then as they sat in the cart, looking back at the house, she had Karen hold the computer.

A creepy sensation crawled over Lainie's neck and shoulders. Was someone watching her? She scanned the tree line along the front of the property but didn't find anything unusual. She glanced toward the house, then at the cottage and barn areas. Again, there wasn't an explanation for the creeps.

With a nervous exhale, she shook off the feeling.

"So, here's what I'm thinking," Lainie said, showing Karen the images on the computer. "I'll put six lighted Christmas trees along the entrance drive. I'll use all white lights. Very elegant-looking."

"Very sparkly," Karen said.

Lainie held out the pocket watch, picturing the trees in her mind's eye. In a swish of light, the trees appeared. Plus, there was a sound of something dropping softly in the tin box. Lainie looked inside. Six tree cookies with tiny silver balls peeked up at her from inside the container.

Lainie sighed. "Everything I make also comes to me in cookie form. I'm not sure what I'm doing wrong."

Karen selected a cookie and took a bite. "That's okay. Cookies are a good thing."

"Not when that's not what I'm going for."

"What's next?"

Lainie drove the cart up the driveway halfway to the house. She tapped the computer keys to scroll to the next image she'd saved. "Angels or a sleigh and reindeer?"

Karen leaned in to get a closer look. "Sleigh and reindeer."

"Got it." She extended her hand, and the timepiece glowed as she envisioned the lighted sleigh and reindeer on the lawn. She didn't close her eyes, but focused her attention on every detail, from the hooves and antlers to the reins linking them together, to the sleigh and sack of toys filling the back. It all appeared with circles of light and a swirl of mist.

"No cookies," Karen said. "I think you're getting the hang of this."

"I hope so."

She changed the image on the computer screen to one of a house decked out in lights with every roof line and window outlined. This was a huge projection, the largest she'd tried so far. It required a lot of energy. Lainie maintained her focus until it was complete.

"There." When the glow of the talisman stopped, she sank back into the seat of the cart.

"You did it. Beautiful. I can't wait to see it all at night when the twinkle of lights will truly shine," Karen said enthusiastically.

Lainie still felt like someone or something watched. Could it be Sarah and her friends? She didn't see anything. Was Sarah capable of being invisible? Perhaps she was being influenced by too many superhero movies.

Lainie shifted her attention. "Two more and I'm done. I want to light up the cottage and barn."

She went through the same process with those buildings, covering them with white lights.

"This place will be lit up like a beacon," Karen said.

"I guess that's the point, to attract business. To let people know we're here." Lainie smiled.

"Well, this will certainly do it. How are you going to turn them on and off? Magic?" Karen asked.

Lainie shrugged. "I haven't thought about that. Maybe I'll just leave them on."

"I'd hate to see your electric bill."

"It's only through the holidays."

"Does the magic last? Or does it have a time limit?" Karen asked.

"I'm not really sure. I guess we'll find out." Lainie closed the laptop, then started the golf cart. "Hey, would you like to stay for dinner? Kalen's grilling pork chops."

"That would be wonderful. Beats heating up leftovers. Hubs has a Rotary Club meeting tonight. You should think about joining that, with the winery business now and all."

"Maybe in time. I have enough to keep me occupied for a while. I have a lot to learn." Charlie would teach her about the winery business. But who would guide her in the magic? Or was she simply expected to learn on her own?

When Lainie and Karen entered the kitchen, Kalen stood at the counter prepping dinner. Her heart fluttered. Her strapping bodyguard chopped potatoes, onions, and red bell peppers, placing them in a roasting pan. Well, he wasn't exactly hers, was he?

And yet he was. He was here specifically to protect her. She liked having him around and needed to remind herself that he would eventually return to where he'd come from.

He was not hers to keep. Perhaps she should think of him as just a dragon shifter. Like, who fell in love with a dragon?

She gave herself a mental shake. No. What she felt wasn't love, just fascination.

"I'm getting better," she announced to him. "I didn't create nearly as many cookies."

He chuckled. The pleasant rumble reverberated in the house. "That's great."

Temporary. *This was only temporary*, she reminded herself. Something must have shown in her expression. Karen raised a questioning brow. Lainie lifted a shoulder and let it fall.

"Yes. My use of magic seems to be improving. Karen's staying for dinner."

"Super." He peered at Karen. "Lainie complains that I make enough to feed an army."

"You do."

"Aye. But I like leftovers."

"Hmph. The kids will be home from school shortly. Anything I can do to help?"

"No. Why don't you and Karen pour a glass of wine and relax on the patio?" He opened the oven, placed the veggies inside, and stood brandishing an oven mitt. OMG. There was something sexy about a man who cooked.

He reached for a bottle of wine on the counter and a wine opener. "Here. Try this. Charlie sent over a case. It's the vineyard's reserve wine. It's rather good."

"I hope it's good. I have to admit, I was caught up in the romance of a winery. I hadn't considered whether the wine was good or not."

"That's okay. There are ways to improve the wine," Karen said.

"I suppose," Lainie agreed.

Kalen passed two glasses of wine across the counter. "Now. Out of the kitchen."

Lainie laughed. It must be a cook's thing. She'd heard that phrase numerous times before from her mom.

Lainie and Karen found seats on the patio, watching the wispy clouds in the sky turn orange and lavender as dusk settled.

Brennon and Jenna came bounding in. "I love the Christmas lights," Jenna said, tickled with enthusiasm. "They'll look even better when it's completely dark."

"Yeah. It looks great," Brennon added. "How'd you get all that done today? What'd you do, hire a crew?"

"There are people who do that as their business. They work magic, don't they?" Lainie finished her wine in one long sip.

Karen shot her a look.

Kalen strolled onto the patio and lit the gas grill. "Dinner will be ready in twenty minutes," he announced.

On his next pass, when he brought out the pork chops on a platter ready to grill, he dropped the wine bottle on the table. "A second glass?"

"With dinner," Lainie said, rising from her seat. "I'll set the table."

"I'll help," Karen added.

Kalen cleared his throat. "By the way, I invited Charlie. I hope you don't mind."

Lainie glanced from Kalen to Karen and spoke to them in a low tone. "No talking about magic. Got it."

"What about the Magic?" Brennon asked from the kitchen. "I've been wanting to get game tickets."

Lainie blinked, following the shift in the conversation. "Oh, the Orlando Magic. Which game is that?"

"Huh?"

"Who are they playing?" Lainie asked.

"Oh. The LA Lakers at the end of the month."

"Maybe you should ask Santa for tickets," she teased.

"Uh, yeah."

She walked past him on her way to the dining room to set the table. Karen was right behind her. Lainie got the plates and silverware out of the cabinet, set them on the table, then fetched the placemats and napkins.

"Maybe Kalen would like to go," Brennon said, glancing to the patio.

"We'll talk with him about it, okay?" If he was still with us, that is.

The doorbell rang. "I'll get it," Lainie said, heading for the front door with Bitsy following at her heels. She let Charlie in. Bitsy did her little hello dance.

"Hi. I'm glad you could make it."

He handed her a bottle of wine. "This one isn't one of ours but was a favorite of Suzie's."

"Oh. Thank you. Let's have some with dinner."

He nodded. "I thank Kalen, and you, for the invitation," Charlie said.

"Just so you know, we're not going to talk about magic in front of the kids. It's a secret," Lainie whispered, then scooped Bitsy up with one hand in order to keep her from bothering him.

Charlie nodded. "No problem."

"What would you like to drink?" Lainie asked Charlie.

"I'm good for now. I'll have wine with dinner."

Kalen waved from the porch and Charlie strolled out to greet him. When Lainie joined Karen in the dining room, her friend already had everything finished. "Thanks for setting the table," Lainie told Karen.

"You're welcome. I like the red placemats."

Lainie chuckled, then set the pup on the floor. "They were an Amazon purchase. Before I realized I could conjure what I wanted."

"Good deal. Maybe you want to save your, um, talent for important things."

Lainie shrugged. "Maybe." Was it limited? There was still so much she didn't know.

"Ready to eat?" Kalen said as he peered around the corner from the kitchen.

"Oh yes," Lainie said. It was wonderful to have someone else cook. "Brennon, can you help bring the food to the table? Everyone, find a seat."

Lainie went into the kitchen to help gather the dishes. Brennon and Kalen had done a fine job of assembling serving dishes and had everything under control. They carried the food into the dining room and took their places. "This looks fabulous," Lainie said.

"Thank you. I'm happy to contribute something and make your day a little easier," he said.

Lainie knew he had been trying to fit in and feel useful since being here. She could understand that. A bodyguard spent a lot of time waiting around for something to happen. Right?

Lainie smiled. "This is a super meal for a weeknight. Watch out, or you'll spoil us." She started passing around the roasted vegetables, followed by pork chops, a slaw salad, and rolls. There was an assortment of wines to choose from, including the one Charlie had brought. Everyone dug in, and conversation lulled.

"The Christmas decorations you did out front are beautiful," Charlie said.

"Thank you. Karen and I had fun with that."

Karen finished chewing and added. "I was just along for the ride."

"Yeah, Mom. I can't believe you got it done in one day," Brennon said. "That was a great crew."

She nodded, busying herself with chewing. Kalen and Lainie shared a glance. She wanted to change the subject. A tinge of guilt nagged at her. Maybe she should tell them about the magic, so she didn't have to come up with stories. "So, is everything set for the wedding Saturday?" she asked Charlie.

"Yes. Although I'm not in on every detail. That's up to my niece and the planner. But they assured me they had it under control."

"When I spoke to Marianne, she seemed very professional. I'm curious to see how this goes. We could use her as a regular planner," Lainie said. It would be fun to host the weddings without being bogged down in the details.

"Maybe you can find a time when the girls can come over," Karen said. "They're anxious to see the place."

"Yeah. Sure. Let's do a group text and see when everyone is free. I'm not actually involved with the wedding, so pretty much any time is open for me."

"Okay. I'll message everyone. With the holidays, who knows, it may not happen until January." Karen chuckled.

"That's life in the fast lane," Lainie said. Although her calendar wasn't full. But she'd be busy with the house and vineyard.

"Mom, I have a couple of job prospects I'm checking out on Saturday. So I won't be around," Brennon said.

Jenna studied her brother. "Maybe you could drop me off at Sela's." She glanced at her mom. "There's nothing I have to do here, right? I'm going to see if she wants to go to the mall."

"Well..." Lainie hesitated. They were all into doing their own thing. She needed to get used to that. "Check it out with Sela and her mom, and then we'll see."

"Great." Jenna's smile reached her eyes. It was nice to see her happy.

"What's for dessert?" Brennon asked.

Kalen collected his plate and stood. "That's your mother's department. Although I understand she's done pretty well with Christmas cookies."

"Mom, you're holding out on me," Brennon said.

She laughed. "The cookie tin is in the pantry. You can get it and bring it to the table."

"Mmm. Homemade cookies. I haven't had those is a long while," Charlie said.

"They aren't anything special," Lainie said. Not homemade, either.

"My Suzie used to make these cookies that she squeezed out of a tube. All different colors and shapes. They were my favorite."

"It sounds like she used a cookie press," Karen said.

"Yes. I think that's it. She called them Scandinavian cookies, I think," Charlie added.

"I'll have to try to make some of those," Lainie said.

Brennon passed the Christmas tin, taking a couple for himself.

"If you do, I'll buy some from you," Charlie said.

"I don't sell cookies," Lainie laughed. "I'll be happy to make you a batch."

Kalen, Brennon, and Jenna had cleared the table. "Just leave the dishes. I'll do them. Maybe you guys would like to hang out on the patio. It's such a lovely evening."

"I hate to eat and run," Karen said, "but hubs will be home from his meeting soon, and I've been gone since early afternoon. I may need to feed and let the dog out."

"I know what that's like." As if on cue, Bitsy trotted into the room. Lainie walked Karen to the door.

"Bye, everyone. It was a lovely dinner. Thank you," Karen said from the entryway.

There was a round of farewells. Lainie continued with Karen outside.

"Oh, the lights turned out stunning," Karen said.

"They did." Lainie took a moment to admire them. She strolled with Karen down the sidewalk to her car. "Thanks for your help today. It was great to have some company."

"You're welcome. Anytime. I'll let you know when we can have a girls' day. Kay?"

"Okay. Take care." She watched as Karen drove down the driveway, between her rows of lit Christmas trees, and onto the street.

She inhaled the cool night air, admiring the twinkling lights. It had been a wonderful day.

CHAPTER NINETEEN

What Goes Up, Must Come Down

WHEN SHE RETURNED TO the new house after taking Jenna to school, Lainie dropped her purse on the kitchen table and stared at the pile of mail that she'd ignored over the past week. She'd had John's mail forwarded to her, and she knew diving into the underbelly of his life wasn't going to be fun. She swallowed a lump of dread.

There would be demons to face.

But it had to be done.

If there were ever a time she wished she could use magic to deal with something, this would be it. Poof, and the entire mess would be gone.

Life didn't work that way, though. She carried the stack, along with a letter opener, out to the deck and dumped it on the table. At least she'd have a pleasant view. She went back inside to get something to drink. Grabbing a coke from the fridge, she also eyed a generous helping of German chocolate cake. Fortification.

At least it wasn't fornication. She snickered as she sat, taking a bite of cake before she began. That would be right up John's alley.

Along that line of thinking, she wondered how many times he'd cheated on her. Maybe half a dozen. Maybe more. Who knew? And how many times had she cheated on him? Zero.

The image of Kalen, naked after he'd shifted, came to mind. Book boyfriends didn't count. Her lips tugged into a smile. She ate another bite of yummy cake.

A good way to take the edge off a crappy task.

Oh my. She needed to get ahold of herself.

She opened all the envelopes and separated them by type: regular bills, credit-card bills, doctor bills, and other. The junk mail and empty envelopes she discarded.

She'd been reveling in the excitement of the move into the new house and the romance of the winery and upcoming wedding. It had been easy to push this task off. Along with going to the trailer. She needed to do that, too. For one thing, she wanted to pick up the boxes of Christmas decorations. Then, she also should straighten up the place before taking the kids there. Not looking forward to that. Maybe she could delay that until after the holidays.

Lainie leaned back and drank her soda. It had been just under two weeks since John's passing, she reminded herself. Her lawyer had said it would take about sixty days for the insurance settlement to be paid.

She stacked the papers into a pile, deciding to deal with it all once that payment came in, when she could use that money. Way to procrastinate.

She heard the door to the garage click shut, followed by a shuffle of feet from the kitchen. She glanced over her shoulder. Kalen had come in from his morning surveillance run. At least that's what she'd dubbed it. He seemed to have settled into a routine of scouting the grounds in the morning.

She wasn't sure why. Perhaps just to have something to do. But he'd been more vigilant since the visit by the evil trio, becoming her shadow. It made her feel like he expected something to happen at any time. "Are we safe?" she asked.

"For now."

Lainie shivered. That implied they wouldn't be at some point. "I need to go to John's trailer. Want to tag along?"

"Tag?" he questioned.

"Come with me," she explained. There were idioms he didn't get, but he was doing better. Watching TV programs helped. She stood and gathered the stack of papers.

"Oh. Yes. That would be a good idea." He got a Gatorade out of the fridge and turned, twisting off the lid. Chinchy sat on his shoulder. He gave the chinchilla a pinch of lettuce.

"Okay. We'll leave in a few minutes." She went upstairs, passing Sawyer resting in his new favorite spot, sunning in the windowsill overlooking the front entrance. "We're going out," she said to the cat.

"I heard," Sawyer drawled. "Perhaps you can pick me up some treats. Catnip or something?"

She laughed. "I'll add it to my shopping list."

"Much appreciated."

Lainie made a pit stop, then paused in the closet to get money out of the duffle bag. She still hadn't picked up a safe. Now that this was her permanent residence, she should at least get a portable one. She dragged her phone from her pocket and added it to her list.

If it didn't make it on her list, she'd forget. Perhaps she should look into those memory meds they advertised on TV. She snorted.

Downstairs again, she put the money in her purse. "Ready?" she called to Kalen.

He strolled from his room. "Lead the way."

Forty minutes later, she pulled into the driveway. She turned off the van, gripping the steering wheel to ground herself. Maybe she wasn't ready to be here. The last time, she'd been in a hurry to get the timepiece box and get out. There hadn't been time to wallow in the past.

"Are you okay?" Kalen asked.

"Yeah. Sure."

"This is where you lived?" he asked as if it wasn't what he'd expected.

"For nearly seventeen years." She opened her car door and got out. He did the same.

They walked together up the steps to the small wooden deck. Her hand shook as she took the keys from her purse and unlocked the door. She inhaled a deep breath, held it, then let it out.

Memories flooded her brain as she stepped inside. It seemed like so long ago that she'd lived here. She reminded herself that it had only been a couple of months. But so much had changed.

"What can I do to help?" Kalen broke into her thoughts.

"I...I don't know." She moved through the living room, not much different there, and into the kitchen. Everything had been left, frozen in time. A half-eaten sandwich sat on a paper plate on the counter. Glasses filled the sink.

She strolled into the bedroom, stopping short. Paper wrappers the paramedics had used littered the floor. Everything had been left as it was the night he'd died. The bed was unmade, a woman's nightgown among the sheets. Lainie pressed the back of her hand against her mouth. Her eyes watered. She swallowed. "I had imagined coming back would be hard. But I hadn't expected this."

"We can do it another time. You don't have to deal with this now," he said, touching her shoulder.

"Yes. I do. I need to put this behind me." She gave herself a shake, walked into the kitchen, and plucked several trash bags from the cabinet. Handing one to Kalen, she said, "You start with the stuff the paramedics discarded on the floor. I'll handle the rest. We're not going to get through all this today."

Lainie stripped the bed linens, stuffing everything in a bag. Kalen picked up all the discarded medical wrappings on the floor and then moved to the kitchen. "We'll need to empty the refrigerator," she called out to him. "Fortunately, there's probably not much in there."

An hour and a half later, they'd dealt with the most critical items and put four bags of trash at the curb for pickup. Lainie got a box of Christmas ornaments from the top of the bedroom closet. These were the ornaments that held a special place in her heart. Lots of memories. There were other decorations stored in the shed outside, but nothing of importance. She took two boxes of photos from under the bed and added them to the small collection in the van.

That was it. She had taken all she wanted. The rest, except for any items the kids may want, could go to Goodwill. She closed the front door and locked it. *If* she brought the kids back here, it wouldn't be until after the holidays.

She turned, the feeling of being watched making the hairs on her neck stand on end. She glanced around. No one was there. "Do you feel that?" she asked Kalen.

He peered sideways at her. "That's the sensation of magic." He put his hand on his hip. Did he have a knife hidden there?

"I've felt it before. Outside of the house," she said.

"So have I. Whoever it is, they're leaving an imprint of magic. That tells me they're immensely powerful."

"How dangerous do you think they are?"

He shrugged. "I'm not sure. They want the timepiece. I don't think they'll try anything unless they're sure they can get it. Fairies and the like are sneaky and cautious creatures. They won't confront you unless they think they have the upper hand."

"So I need to project strength?"

"I would say so."

"Survival of the fittest," she muttered.

Lainie stared at John's truck. Sadness filled her heart. Brennon could use the truck, she supposed, but really, she didn't want the constant reminder of John. Better to sell it and get Brennon something new. Maybe for Christmas.

She strolled to her shiny red van. It was amazing what the magical money could do. She was so thankful.

CHAPTER TWENTY

Cheers

FRIDAY AFTERNOON, THE DECORATING crew for the wedding arrived. Lainie didn't have to do anything, but she checked periodically to see how the setup was going. The weather was perfect, a clear and cool December day in Florida.

A crew set white folding chairs on the lawn. A focal point was created with two huge interlocking rings, seeming made of wood and assembled near the lake. Flowers in hues of lavender, rose, and yellow were added.

The dinner area consisted of a dozen round tables. Poles were hammered into the ground to support a lacework of tiny lights overhead. The buffet tables were positioned inside the barn.

Lainie spotted Marianne giving instructions. "Hi. It's coming together nicely. I like the way the service will be overlooking the lake."

"Thanks," Marianne said. "We're just laying out the footprint. Tomorrow, we'll do the finishing touches of tablecloths and decorations. Then the food will be brought in, and voila. It will be gorgeous."

"You must love doing this. Weddings are so exciting and beautiful," Lainie said wistfully.

"They are. Each one should be unique and exactly what the bride dreams it should be."

Lainie thought of her own small wedding. Not quite what she'd dreamed of, but neither was her marriage. She forced the memory away.

"Well, good luck. I may pop over for a bit, if that's okay? I won't get in your way."

"That's fine. It's your property. You're always welcome," Marianne said.

"Great. You won't even know I'm here."

Lainie watched from the upstairs window as guests rolled in, filling the grassy area marked off for parking in front of the cottage. The wedding was scheduled to take place at sunset. She hadn't decided whether she'd go over during the ceremony or not. Charlie had encouraged her to come by. But she didn't feel as though she belonged. So, maybe, maybe not.

Besides, the bougie bitches would be arriving at seven for a girls' night. Kalen was playing chef again, fixing an array of yummy grilled foods.

She skipped downstairs and found him already prepping for the evening. Again, a man in the kitchen was so appealing. He grabbed a grill spatula and waggled his brows. Gawd, he was handsome.

Like an author would use an ugly guy in a romance. *Duh.*

Lainie slipped the timepiece over her head, then tucked it inside her blouse. She'd put it on a chain so she'd have it when she didn't carry her purse.

"I'm going to the wedding for a few minutes. The suspense is killing me. Do you want to tag along?"

He frowned in indecision. "No. I still have more to do here. Yell, if you need me."

"As in if a monster is chasing me?" she teased.

"Aye. That." He gave Bitsy a square of cheese.

"That dog is going to get fat. You keep giving her table food."

"She burns it off by going up and down the stairs. Her legs are short." He took some sauces from the fridge.

"I won't be long." She went out through the garage, then walked the distance to the cottage. The guests were seated. Music played. She arrived at the perfect time.

She hung off to the side of the cottage where the bridal party had prepared. The bridesmaids stepped out, wearing gowns in shades of rose, each gown a different style to fit each girl's personality and shape. They lined up to make their walk. The groom and groomsmen entered from the side of the barn, then took their place at the front. The procession began, and the five bridesmaids began their walk down the aisle.

The audience stood.

Charlie's niece, Annabelle, walked out of the cottage and stopped, waiting for the wedding march to begin. The crowd inhaled all at once. The bride was stunning—elegant and graceful. She'd chosen an embellished dress of lace and tulle covered with pearls and beading. The off-the-shoulder perfection had long, tulle sleeves and a sheer tulle overskirt atop a fitted lace gown. It had a deep V bodice front and scooped back.

The sunset and golden hour between day and night created a dreamy backdrop that illuminated her in a romantic glow.

Lainie wished Jenna had stayed home to see this beautiful wedding. Not that she wanted her daughter to marry any time soon, just that perhaps she could set her dreams on something more that she'd had. Her eyes misted.

The ceremony was lovely. Lainie stayed put until the guests rose to leave the seating area. Then she scooted back to the house. With the early sunset hour, she had plenty of time before her friends arrived.

Kalen had wine glasses set out, cheese and crackers, a relish tray, chocolate hummus—a new discovery—and fruit. She felt bad that she'd deserted him with the preparations.

"Sorry I abandoned you. The wedding was spectacular. I'm so thrilled with how the whole thing turned out."

"Nae problem."

"Anything I can do to help?"

"Set out whatever plates you'd like to use."

"Got it." With a variety of place-setting styles to choose from—thankfully, she and Sue evidently had similar tastes—she chose simple, white square plates. She arranged the plates, silverware, and napkins at the end of the counter closest to the deck.

Sawyer came bounding down the stairs. "They're here." Lainie chuckled. Who needed—the doorbell—when they had a cat like Sawyer?

Lainie opened the door. "Hey. Welcome."

The group filed in, each gal giving Lainie a quick hug as they entered. Lainie still treasured those hugs.

"Awesome lawn decorations," Picku said.

"I never made it over to your rental place, but this," Shreena said, turning in a circle to gaze up at the high ceiling, "is fabulous. Congrats."

"Thanks. There's a selection of wines on the counter. A few from this winery."

"Cool," Nandita said. "I'll start with one of those." She walked straight to the wine display.

"Try the rosé in the chiller. It's particularly good," Lainie said.

"Hi, Kalen." Alaina waved a hand. He lifted the spatula in acknowledgment. Then she faced Lainie. "So, how's the wedding going?"

"It's spectacular. Marianne, the wedding planner, did a terrific job. The bride is gorgeous. Her dress is to die for. She looks like a fairy princess," Lainie said.

"That's something, given we've met a real fairy princess," Karen added.

"Not fair. Shreena, Nandita, and I weren't there for that. I declare a do-over. I want to see the fairy land," Picku said.

They each poured the wine of their choice. Karen raised her glass in a toast. "To new adventures." The gals clinked their glasses together before drinking.

Kalen carried in platters from the grill.

"Thank you," Lainie said, holding his gaze a second longer than necessary. "Okay, ladies, we have slider burgers, bacon-wrapped shrimp, and BBQ wings."

"Mmm. Looks delicious. Good thing I ate a light lunch," Picku said. Then she tipped her head toward Lainie, lowering her voice. "Is he the one who turns into a dragon?"

Lainie glared at Alaina.

"You know me. When something excites me, I talk," Alaina admitted.

"I forgive you," Lainie said. "But don't forget he's fictional." Something she often had to remind herself of. He was growing on her, big time.

Everyone dug into the food and wine. "Grab a plate, Kalen," Lainie said.

He did. Sawyer sauntered in, jumping onto the stool so he wouldn't be at floor level. Karen fixed him a small plate of cheese and bacon-covered shrimp. "Thanks, sweetheart," he said.

Karen and Alaina already knew that the cat could talk and shift into a human. Lainie had only seen him do it when in the fairy universe. The other gals thought his speaking was a great novelty. And it was, but Lainie expected it now.

After they'd eaten, Lainie gave them a tour of the house. When they peered out the windows, they could see the reception going on next door at the winery. "They're dancing and having a good time. Let's dash over and take a look. I'm sure they won't notice us," Alaina said.

"I don't know," Lainie protested. They were heading downstairs again.

"We'll be good. I'll keep tabs on the wild one," Picku volunteered.

Karen headed for another glass of wine. "I want to see the bride's dress."

Nandita held out her glass for a refill. "I love looking."

"Weddings are so romantic," Shreena sighed.

"Okay. We'll go over for fifteen minutes. That's it," Lainie announced. "Kalen, you, too. You're my bodyguard. So, guard my body." She laughed.

"Someone may have had too much wine," Picku said.

"I'm not driving." Lainie led them through the front door, along the sidewalk to the wedding celebration. "We're not crashing the wedding. Just a peek and then back to the house."

CHAPTER TWENTY-ONE

What's With The Vertigo?

THE BRIDE AND HER husband were on the dance floor, performing a choreographed dance together. OMG, Lainie's heart fluttered, wishing to have a guy like that. It was probably every dance teachers' dream to have that kind of guy. She glanced over at Kalen, thinking that never in a million years would he do that.

He seemed to be taking it all in, the way he did with every new thing. A charming expression crossed his face. His eyes met hers, holding her gaze steadily. The intensity caused a shiver to curl down her spine. Then, just as suddenly as the intensity came, it evaporated. He grinned and raised a brow as if the moment hadn't happened.

"I adore her dress," Alaina whispered.

Lainie spotted Charlie, then walked over to him. "It's a beautiful wedding."

"Yes. Suzy would have loved it," he said with a hint of sadness in his voice.

"She's watching. I feel it."

He lifted his chin. "So do I."

Lainie gazed at the couple for a few minutes.

"There's something else, though. Magic. Dark magic. It's nearby. It's coming," Charlie warned.

Lainie snapped her head around to look at him. "Oh no. That can't be good."

Charlie's jaw tightened. "The magic here… it's familiar." His voice dipped low, almost lost beneath the music and laughter spilling from the reception hall. "This isn't the witch's work. The signature is sharper. Cleaner. It cuts instead of spreads." Lainie's eyes widened, but he wasn't finished. "I've only felt it once before, years ago. A collector of relics—some say souls—passed through our territory. Left a trail of missing artifacts and terrified familiars." He looked at her, gaze haunted. "If he's here, he's not here for the party."

She spun on her heel and hurried to Kalen and the gals.

"What's wrong?" Kalen asked.

Lainie felt a little breathless, both from excitement and fear. "We need to go. Charlie thinks dark magic could be—" Something gray flew by her head. A bat? "Come on," she ordered, then ran toward the house.

Something dove at the group again. Several somethings. Shreena squealed.

"Go. Into the house," Lainie said. She stopped and held her ground, batting a hand at the flying creatures. Goblins, she realized. Instantly, the image of the flying monkey creatures from the *Wizard of Oz* came to mind. That had scared the bejeezus out of her as a child. But these were goblins. She spotted Sarah, Wolfie, and what she thought was a nymph near the shadows. Cowards. Always out of reach. Having someone else do their dirty work.

Lainie whipped out the timepiece and flipped it open. There were six of them now, flying over the driveway and along the side of the house.

"Give us the timepiece," Wolfie shouted.

"Give it up," Sarah added. "And I'll call them off."

"Hand it over, or else," the nymph crooned.

Distracted by the trio, she let her guard down. One goblin dove at her as she lifted her arm. Pain seared her arm as it struck her. She jerked backward, lost her balance, and fell, then rolled.

Kalen bent to help her up. The goblins swarmed.

Out of the corner of her eye, she saw Kalen draw his daggers. He lunged for the goblin that had scratched her. Something wet splattered her arm.

Lainie held the talisman up and imagined lightning firing at them. A bolt shot out and hit one then the other, bursting into a fireworks kind of sizzle and burn as it disappeared.

Kalen threw a star, striking one in the chest at the same instant she zapped it. In quick succession, they dispatched the goblins.

As soon as the last was gone, she turned the talisman on Sarah and her cohorts. Lightning fired at them. One by one, they disappeared as if realizing it wasn't safe to hang around.

When it was over, Lainie collapsed against Kalen, grabbing hold of his arm to remain on her feet. "That took a massive amount of energy," she said.

She had reacted faster this time, aimed intentionally — but the magic still came like a flood instead of a blade. Strength without refinement. She'd won, but it had nearly emptied her.

Sawyer crouched beside one of the fallen goblins, frowning as he examined the creatures' eyes. "They weren't acting on instinct," he said. "Something—or someone—was directing them." He rose slowly, brushing off his hands. "Goblins don't gather in groups for attack patterns unless they're under command." He looked at Lainie then, a seriousness settling into his features. "There's only one type of magic that binds swarms like this. Collector magic. It scouts. It tests. It measures the strength of what it's after." His gaze flicked briefly to the timepiece in her hand. "And I think it just measured you."

"No. This is Sarah's doing."

Sawyer tisked. "The witch can't wield this kind of power without help."

Kalen wrapped his arm around her back and held her up. "Let's get you into the house."

"What the heck," Karen said, running to help as Kalen brought her into the house. "Set her on the sofa. Are you hurt?"

"Just a scratch. I'm fine."

After settling Lainie on the sofa, Kalen dashed into the kitchen.

"Damn. That was scary," Picku said.

"I know," Lainie said, leaning back with a deep sigh. "I hope it didn't scare people at the wedding."

"I don't think they could see what was happening. Every time one of the creatures was killed, it burst into what looked like fireworks. So, it may have looked like a fireworks display."

"I thought I heard clapping when it was over," Nandita said.

Kalen returned with a damp cloth and sat next to her, gently wiping her face and arms to remove whatever spattered her when they zapped the goblins. "Okay, ladies, I think we're finished for tonight." He stood, looking quite protective. "Lainie needs to rest. That encounter cost her a lot of energy."

"Of course," Karen said. "We'll follow up another time. Can we help you clean up before we leave?"

"No. Thank you, but it won't take me long," Kalen said, resting a hand on Lainie's shoulder in a stay-here-and-rest gesture before stepping away.

"Thanks for coming," she said, sitting up, but not standing. "I'll be fine in a few minutes."

Kalen walked her friends out.

"Let me know if Lainie needs anything," Alaina said.

"I will," he said from the front porch, then closed the door and turned toward Lainie. "You rest. I'll be right back."

As she slowly lay down, Sawyer hopped onto the sofa and curled up at her feet. She closed her eyes, seeing the goblins behind her lids. They'd defeated them, she reminded herself. They're gone.

It could have been minutes, or hours, she wasn't sure when Kalen returned. "Let's get you to bed."

He slipped his arm beneath hers to help her stand. "Hmm. What do you have in mind?" she asked.

Kalen snort-laughed, which did nothing to assuage her feelings. Did he think she wasn't worthy of him? Or maybe she wasn't as pretty as the heroines in his book. That's it. Book heroes and heroines could be anything the author wanted them to be. As beautiful and virile as...

She must be delusional to have feelings for him. He wasn't real.

Oh, but he felt very real. She squeezed her hand over his firm arm muscles. Yes, real.

When they got to the kitchen, her legs nearly gave way. "You cleaned the kitchen. You should have waited. I would have help."

At the bottom the stairs, he swooped her into his arms and carried her up to her bedroom. Setting her down next to the bed and steadying her with one arm, he tugged the sheets aside. "Have your way with me, my lord," she muttered.

Then she tossed her arm over her eyes. "I don't know if it's the wine, or the fight, but I'm sooo exhausted."

There was a long silence.

"Would you stay with me? I don't want those winged monkeys to get in."

Later, when the house had gone still and the night wrapped gently around her, Lainie slipped a hand over the pocket watch, needing reassurance more than anything. Her fingertips brushed the timepiece—and a muted shimmer of sensation rippled outward, like touching the surface of a pond disturbed by a faraway pebble. A hush filled her ears, not silence but an awareness, as though something distant had just turned its attention fully toward her. Lainie drew a breath and let her hand fall away. Whatever was searching... it had found her trail.

Sometime well before daylight, Lainie woke. She was bone tired, but she had to pee, and she'd just had the weirdest dream. Kalen had rescued her.

When she rolled to get out of bed, and her hand struck something hard. She patted it. Hair. But it didn't feel like Bitsy. She sat too quickly, groaned, and peered through the darkness. Enough light filtered through the window for her to make out Kalen's sleeping form.

He'd stayed with her. Just as she'd asked. She vaguely recalled that part of last evening. Actually, she remembered it all. Her face flushed hotly. She'd no doubt made a fool of herself.

Well, no matter. It was sweet of him to stay and look after her.

She went to the bathroom. Then she padded down the hall to check on the kids to make sure they were both home and in bed. She peeked in Jenna's room first, then Brennon's. They were both sound asleep.

What time was it anyway? Back in her room, she checked the clock. Three thirty-five. She slipped back under the covers, pulling them over her shoulders.

When she woke in the morning, she found him staring at her. She blinked. "Thank you for staying with me," she said.

He cupped her jaw in his big hand, then ran his thumb over her cheekbone. "Nae problem."

His version of "no problem" was totally growing on her. She smiled.

He frowned, abruptly rising from the bed. "I'll go fix us some coffee."

"It's Sunday. The kids don't have school, so there's no hurry."

"I know. I'll have it ready for you when you come downstairs." He strolled out of the bedroom.

She sighed, grinning. That had been one of the sweetest things she'd ever heard.

CHAPTER TWENTY-TWO

Unexpected Gifts

LAINIE DRIFTED INTO THE kitchen with the hangover from hell. She paused at the counter, placing her fingers on her temples, trying to rub away the ache. Either she'd had too much wine last night or the fray she'd encountered with the goblins had done her in. The deadly trio—Sarah, the witch, Wolfie, and a nymph she hadn't yet been introduced to—had been calling the shots of the goblin attack. They'd remained in the shadows pulling the strings while Lainie and Kalen fought off the creatures.

Kalen pushed the Keurig top shut to start her coffee. She winced as the click of it engaging sounded far louder than usual.

"That bad, huh?" Kalen asked.

"Yeah. Not feeling my best this morning? And the place on my arm where the goblin scratched me last night is swollen and painful." She raised her arm to look at the red gash.

Sawyer jumped onto the counter and peered at her arm. "You need to soak that in a tea solution. Goblins have venomous spurs on their hind legs. If that's what caught you, then that's most likely why you're not feeling well. It isn't too much wine, as you thought. It's goblin poisoning."

"Poisoning?" Kalen said, worried. "I'll prepare tea bags."

"What kind of poisoning? Is it like a bee sting, spider, or snake?" She tried to think of venomous creatures. She propped her elbow on the counter, holding her chin in her hand. Her head felt heavy. Her eyes drifted shut."

"I'm not sure. Maybe closer to a bee sting. Although I remember something about a bird having a similar effect just from holding it. I think it was due to the type of beetle it ate." Sawyer's words faded.

She jerked, experiencing the sensation of falling, then blinked.

"Give us the timepiece. Give it up, or else?" That was what the trio had said before they'd disappeared. Or else what? She hadn't said. Lainie would turn into a three-eyed monster? They'd keep harassing her? What did that mean? Consequences. Everything had consequences. They'd already stepped through a portal into another fairy dimension.

Magic came with a price.

Kalen gently lifted her arm and positioned it across the counter, placing a towel beneath it. Looking at her, he explained, "I don't want to make a mess on your new counter."

Her lips tugged from a smile to a wince. Like that mattered when her arm was swollen, red, and throbbing with pain.

He set a row of four tea bags wet with hot water over the wound. "There. Sit still and let those work their magic."

At the mention of magic, Lainie mused, "I wonder if I could use the timepiece to heal it and remove any poison."

"I don't think it works that way," Sawyer muttered.

"Just my luck," she grumbled. She had a powerful talisman, yet she couldn't control it.

"How does it feel?" Kalen asked, hopeful.

"It's only been a couple of minutes." She stared at him. He was quite impatient at times. Lainie glanced at her arm. "The pain is subsiding."

He nodded. "Good. Just chill."

Lainie blinked. "Chill? Look at you with the lingo."

"The TV is an excellent teacher."

"Huh. Which is why I monitored what my children watched when they were growing up."

"Well, it paid off. They seem to be doing well. I'm glad to see Brennon doing so well in his fighting class."

"Taekwondo." She was not encouraging him to fight but to learn discipline.

"And I think Jenna is learning grace and balance through her dance." He gave a half-smile, seeming pleased with himself.

Lainie chuckled. Since when did he pay so much attention to the kids? "Maybe you should watch a class or two. I'm not sure how much grace comes from her hip-hop class."

He frowned. "Like the kids on YouTube?"

"They're not all kids. Some of them are in their forties and fifties." *In her age group*, she thought with a sigh. "Hey. Are you trying to distract me by talking about the kids." *This must be bad*.

He shrugged. "Well, she is a good daughter."

Lainie nodded. "Of course she is. She's a teenager. She just has her ups and downs, especially after her dad died. The kids tend to romanticize his memory, forgetting the bad times." Like all the times he beat her. Then again, Lainie had tried to shelter them from that. Her thoughts were getting cloudy. Why were they discussing the kids?

She moved her arm and grimaced in pain.

"So how long do I have to keep the tea bags on?" she asked the cat.

"I would suppose until the redness is gone." Sawyer turned and jumped from the counter, trotting over to his food bowl. He made a throat-clearing sound. "Breakfast, please."

Lainie closed her eyes again. She could hear Kalen and Sawyer speaking, but she couldn't make it out. She tried to say something, but the words came out jumbled. What was happening to her?

"Lainie? Lainie?" A paw tapped her cheek. "Kalen, I think she's passed out."

She hadn't. She heard them, but she couldn't open her eyes or speak. Ever since getting out of bed, her body had grown heavier, more lethargic. Was the poison slowly paralyzing her? Even the sense of panic within her seemed sluggish.

Then she thought of the kids, forcing her body to move. One arm slid off the counter and hung limp.

Kalen dashed around the counter, leaning his face close to hers. She could feel his breath on her, but she couldn't open her eyes. "Lainie?" he called, shaking her shoulder.

When she didn't respond, he lifted her and carried her upstairs to her bed. "She just needs rest."

Who was he speaking to? Sawyer? Her body was limp as he laid her on the bed. Then she felt him place something in her hands, positioning it over her breastbone. She moved her fingers ever so slightly. The metal felt warm and familiar. The timepiece.

"Perhaps the timepiece will heal you," Kalen said.

Her heart sputtered like a candle flickering before it went out. She concentrated on the talisman. Still, she could barely control it with her limited faculties. How would this help? She tried to steady her racing heart, telling herself she was overreacting.

She heard Kalen's footsteps retreat. *No. Don't go.* A few minutes later, he returned. She felt him gently lift her arm, then place it back down. Was that a towel? His fingers brushed her arm as he set fresh tea bags on the wound. She imagined herself leaning into him, clinging to the comfort of his company.

"I'm hoping a layer of fresh tea bags will draw more poison out. What else can we do?" Kalen asked worriedly.

"Call on some witches?" Sawyer said.

"I don't know any witches. I don't know anyone in this realm." Kalen paused. "But she needs help. Maybe I should call her friends. Or Brennon? Or Charlie? Yes, Charlie is from a magical people. Maybe he knows something that will stop the poison. I'm going to get him."

She wanted to yell, *No, don't leave*. Right now, it felt like she would never escape the darkness and the suffocating feeling of heaviness. Fear sliced into her belly as she started to doubt her chances of making it through this.

What would the kids do if they lost their mother, too?

In what seemed like seconds later, footsteps pounded the stairs. A breathless Kalen and Charlie burst into the room. She focused on their labored breathing. "He has a medicinal cream that may help," Kalen sputtered.

"What sort of trouble did you get into, girl?" Charlie asked in a soothing voice. "Kalen, remove the tea bags and then use this drawing salve."

Lainie felt Kalen working on her arm to remove the tea bags, then slather on the ointment. The pressure of his fingers sent shooting pains through her forearm and up into her shoulder.

She moaned, or maybe she just imagined the sound. She concentrated on the talisman.

Her hands suddenly heated with power. Energy skipped between her fingers as she felt the timepiece come to life. Magic coiled through her from head to toe, and it was as if she could feel the poison being drawn from her body. Her hands tightened on the timepiece, making sure she remained connected.

"She's doing it," Sawyer said eagerly. "She's using the magic of the timepiece to heal."

She wasn't guiding it—she was surrendering to it. Another lesson then: some magic demanded strength, others demanded vulnerability.

As she opened her eyes and regained her sight, she found Kalen standing close by. Charlie stood at the foot of the bed, and Sawyer sat on her other side, one paw on her left knee.

Relief poured over her. She wasn't going to die, wasn't going to leave Brennon and Jenna behind. Tears burned her eyes as she realized Kalen had come through for her.

He'd cared enough to go the extra distance. What a new concept. His golden eyes took her in from head to toe, and his mouth pulled up at one side, revealing the dimple in his right cheek. "Glad to have you back."

The burning pain in her arm eased. "Yeah. Note to self—don't mess with goblins again."

Kalen's jaw tightened. "Or use your weapon more effectively."

Lainie forced herself up onto her elbows, half sitting. She suppressed a warning shiver. Now that she knew the danger, she wouldn't allow it to happen again.

Charlie stepped back, crossing his arms. "Your color has returned. I think you'll do fine now. I'll leave you to rest."

"Thank you for your help," Lainie said, then Kalen added his thanks.

Sawyer hopped to the floor. "I'll walk you out," the cat said.

The mattress gave as Kalen sat beside her, slipping his strong arm around her to draw her close so she could lean on his shoulder. "I'm sorry. I didn't know goblins could do this, or I would have warned you."

"It's okay. I'm okay." Fear took hold of her at the close call she'd experienced. She realized with clarity the lengths someone would go to to get their hands on the timepiece.

"You need to take it easy and rest," Kalen said, brushing her hair behind her shoulders.

"I will. I'm feeling much better now. I'm even craving a slice of chocolate cake."

He chuckled. "Ah. That's a good sign."

She grinned. "Everything is better with chocolate."

Thank you!

Thanks for reading!

I hope you enjoyed the adventure!

Want to stay up-to-date on upcoming books, release dates,
Giveaways, contests, and extra goodies from me?
Sign up for my NEWSLETTER.
www.larissaemerald.com/newsletter

If you have time to leave a review, I'd appreciate it, and of course, if you
have any friends who love paranormal romance, I hope you tell them
about the book.

Sample of FOREVER

Read on to enjoy a sample of book 1 of

FOREVER

The Terror, MN Series, prequel

Where paranormal creatures like to walk on the wild side.

by

Larissa Emerald

Man, if I could have that kind of money when I'm forty, that would be sweet.

David Snyder straightened the pens and sticky notes on his desk, and adjusted the picture frame holding Abby's photo, his gaze drifting to the Bradley file next to it. The guy had millions. With that kind of dough, he could give her whatever she wanted. A vacation home on Lake Michigan. Three boats. Expensive jewelry. A Louis Vuitton purse. That was the rage with obscenely wealthy clients. He stood.

"Heading to lunch?" Sam asked.

"Yeah."

"Any place in particular?"

"I'm meeting Abby at Bud's Burgers." David knew what was coming next.

"Ooo. Bring me back a burger, huh? I'm swamped." Sam reached for his wallet.

"Come on, man. I'm meeting my girl. I may not even remember to get extra food."

"It's not always about you, Dave," Sam said. "I could eat an entire pig and cow right now. Can't you hear my stomach growling?"

"Actually, it *is* always about me. Hey, if you're overloaded with clients, I'll take a couple off your hands," David half-joked. He worked hard and pushed himself hard. How else would he achieve his professional goal of owning an investment firm by age forty? He had just five more years to make it happen.

Sam rolled his eyes. "Yeah, right."

David hesitated. "Okay...okay. Who else wants something from Bud's Burgers?" he said to the room at large. He usually didn't ask, but knowing he was meeting Abby for lunch put him in an excellent mood.

A chorus of nope, no-thank-you, and none-for-me responses drifted to him. He donned his suit jacket that he'd hung over the back of his chair.

Sam said, "Way to step up. I'll take a burger topped with mac-n-cheese and onion crisps."

Becky chimed in, "Listen to your heart, Sam. It's begging you to get a salad."

"Ugh. Salad at a burger joint? No way." Sam made a disgusted grunt. "I plan on living well while I can." He pulled out a twenty and waved it for David to take.

"We'll settle up when I get back," David said.

On the ground floor, he exited the elevator into the hall and out the double doors onto the busy Chicago sidewalk. It was mid-week following Easter, and the weather was clear and sunny yet a breezy forty-five degrees. It would be a nippy five-block walk.

David pulled his phone from his pocket and checked the time and messages. It was 12:02. Nothing from Abby. He sent her a text. *On my way. Just going to stop and see Tank first. See you in a few.*

David had hired a dog sitter who lived in an older building tucked in amid newer skyscrapers. He usually included a visit during his lunch-hour routine. Well, lunch often took more than an hour, including the twenty-minute or so stop to see Tank, but his job didn't require a time clock.

When Christie opened the door, the Rottweiler dashed over, his stump of a tail wagging furiously, and sat at his feet. "Good boy," David said. He bent and cupped the dog's head between both hands and rubbed.

"How's it going?" David asked.

"Great." Christie looked after three dogs, with Tank the largest among them. The work allowed her to stay at home with her toddler, who padded around in a walker in the living room.

David took Tank out to a small courtyard at the back, grabbing a ball from a toy bin beside the door. The area wasn't large enough for him to toss it and have Tank run around, but the pup loved to play a game of bounce and catch. David believed that if someone had a pet, they should make time for them. So that's what he did. Just like he planned his life around everything else, going to the gym, playing racquetball with Gary, or taking Abby to the theatre, he spent time with Tank. And damn if he didn't love that dog more than he thought possible.

When their fifteen minutes were up, he scrubbed the dog's head and led him inside. "Who's my best buddy?" he said. Since it was

Tuesday, he'd take Tank to the dog park this evening and let him run. "See you later."

He grabbed a hand wipe from the supply that Christie kept on a table beside the door and cleaned his hands, then tossed it into an adjacent wastebasket. "Thanks, Christie," he called across the room. "See ya tonight."

Back on the walk, he fixed his wireless earbuds and set his phone's playlist. Abby's favorite song came on. He smiled, remembering the last time they'd gone clubbing and dancing the night away.

His heart beat faster, anticipating her gorgeous blue eyes, beautiful smile, and lush pink lips. They'd been dating for eight months. The idea of asking her to marry him crept into his mind often lately. Last week, he'd even visited the jewelry store to get ideas for a ring.

He needed to strategize the right romantic moment to bring it together: the ring, a declaration, and popping the question. Should he ask her to be his wife in front of The Bean or arrange a private rooftop dinner where they could slow dance beneath the stars and look over the city lights, or maybe at sunrise at the lake?

Yet even with the love he felt for Abby, it was another woman who was appearing in his dreams of late. She had light brown hair and carried a large purse or bag. She laughed easily. She made him smile, too. But she was always a mystery woman. David didn't have a clue who she was or what his connection to her was.

A shoulder bumped against him as a man hurried past. Startled out of his musings, he turned his attention to navigating the crowded sidewalk as he made his way to the light at the corner. He paused, waiting for the light to turn. A middle-aged woman came up beside him. She had a large pink bag slung over her shoulder. Two furry heads poked out of the front edge of the bag and barked. The annoying black dog that looked more like a rat than a dog strained toward David, his teeth showing as he yapped. The childhood memory of when he'd attended his cousin's baseball game and a feisty dachshund had bitten his lower lip quickly surfaced. That and the subsequent hospital trip for stitches. David took a step backward. Stupid yippy dogs.

The light changed to green, and he gladly outpaced the woman. It had been ages since he'd thought about those days of his youth. He ran his tongue over the thin line of scar tissue along the inside of his lip. Yep, still there.

He needed to turn right and cross the street at the fourth light. Bud's Burgers was a block south. He waited for the crosswalk sign to change. The usual heavy traffic zipped along. Nothing new in this area of downtown. He shoved his hands deep into his pockets as cold air rushed past. A couple across the street caught his attention. They were standing a ways back off the street in a roadside park. He squinted. Abby? She stood with a man. What was she doing with this guy? He gripped her by the arm. A little too forcefully, he thought. She seemed anxious to tug herself free from his hold. Then the man leaned forward and kissed Abby, although she didn't seem happy with the attention. David drew his hands from his pockets, checking the light.

What was going on here? Thoroughly confused, he caught movement in his peripheral vision. People around him started to cross the road.

With his eyes on Abby, he followed the crowd. The beauty shop Abby owned was located on the *other side* of Bud's Burgers. This could not have been a chance meeting with this guy. So what was it? Suddenly, he was aware the people next to him had stopped in the middle of the crosswalk. His gaze darted around to see why. In quick snapshots, he glimpsed a dump truck barreling down the road, and in its path was a young woman pushing a stroller carrying a toddler. The woman froze, eyes wide with terror. The toddler, oblivious to the danger, stared straight at him with the cutest smile on her face. Her brown eyes framed with long lashes were so innocent and playful. Oh shit, no.

His muscles straining, David sprinted toward them. He shoved them back in the direction they'd come from, sending the woman and the stroller carrying the child flying through the air. They landed on top of the people who had stayed on the sidewalk waiting for the truck to pass.

Relief washed over him a second before the sound of screeching tires registered in his brain. The impact of being brutally struck by the dump truck followed. He didn't recall the pain, just a tremendous force sending him airborne, followed by a hard landing. His head cracked against the solid cement curb. Then nothing.

—ele—

Sign up for my NEWSLETTER and read Forever FREE.
LARISSA EMERALD NEWSLETTER

Sample of AWAKENING FIRE

Read on to enjoy a sample of

AWAKENING FIRE

Book 1, The Guardians Series

by

Larissa Emerald

CHAPTER ONE

At the subterranean entrance to the Divine Tree sanctuary, Venn Hearst halted and raised his eyes to the etchings of a wolf and hawk emblazoned in the aged wood above the door, a nod to his alternate forms. Venn extended his tattooed wrist, positioning the elaborately inked tree, and the pulsing artery beneath it, below a glistening twisted root for the anointing ritual. An amber-colored drop of sap spilled over the image, then pooled and bubbled before it was absorbed into his skin, sending a sharp zing to each of his neurons before settling within the larger matching tat on his back.

The language of the universe rustled through the air. The Secrets men died to know, Guardians swore to protect, and the Dark Realms were determined to steal or destroy were housed within this sacred place.

His Divine Tree was one of the original dozen hidden around the globe. There were eleven left after the Divine Tree Guardians had lost his brother Tristan along with the Divine Tree in Germany in the mid-nineteen hundreds. The tree's demise had caused the earth to shift on its axis ever so slightly, bringing them one step closer to Armageddon with an escalation of malevolent forces. Evil had blossomed with Hitler taking millions of lives before balance could be restored. It had been an uphill battle ever since.

Venn opened and closed his fist, considering the tattoo on his wrist. Not even one more tree could be lost.

"Benison," the oak whispered.

"Blessings," Venn returned. "My strength and loyalty are yours."

With his vow, the door to the tree creaked opened, and he strode through the massive entry. He looked around the comfortable above-ground chambers and kept walking. Keeping watch wasn't his intention this night. No, he sought the tombs within the root structure below and hoped the tree would communicate to him if something out of the ordinary was happening.

He grabbed a nearby flashlight from the alcove next to the door, flipped it on, and started along the narrow tunneled path, down a staircase that had been fashioned by twisted knots of wood and roots fused together over centuries. It wound deep into the layers of knowledge, to the catacomb of interconnected scripts, like a true, living computer.

Once in the belly, he ran a hand over an electrical switch. Battery-powered lights illuminate the cave-like room in a pale glow. Venn glanced about and drew an awed breath. *Holy shit. The place had grown.*

With careful steps, he moved from the tunnel into a cavern, where rough splinters jutted out of smooth swirls in the timber's pattern, creating a golden wooden cave. He used to come down here often in the beginning, during the early years of loneliness, always expecting to discover something exceptional. Which he usually did.

He'd learned that if he pricked himself on this special wood, a series of images would fire through his brain, teaching him something new, its lessons sharper and more thorough than those of any history or science channel on TV.

Centuries ago, he'd stumbled on this cavern and its amazing phenomenon quite by accident. The power the tree gave him had become an obsession, the data exchange an addiction. He knew better than to come back again after that. But this time he had no choice, his duty demanded he use every means available to him. He was well aware of the risks and didn't intend to overstep his limits.

Something was off-kilter in the universe, and he needed to know why. The odd weather pattern—winter when it should be spring—was an ominous sign, Venn knew, even if humans simply took it as a fluke of nature. Just as humans showed symptoms of illness, so too did the machinations of the universe. And a shift between good and evil often triggered such nasty weather patterns.

He needed to be on high alert. "Custos," he spoke quietly to the ancient tree. "Do you know what's going on?"

There was no answer.

Taking a seat in a worn cradle of wood, he felt the need to connect with the Divine Tree . . . and to his brothers. He squeezed the back of his neck. Perhaps that's what the problem was. Not outside at all, but within him.

He felt as isolated from everything as this tree was. What was it like to house all humanity but not feel humanity?

The groan and creak of the tree, as if it were caught by a strong gust of wind, caused Venn to lift his head. Seth stood framed in the tunnel doorway. "I didn't think you'd be down here," the angel said, walking into the chamber.

Now Venn *knew* there was trouble brewing. The angel rarely dropped in just to say hello. "What's happenin'?" Venn asked in way of greeting. Seth shrugged, his wings lifting and falling with the movement. "I'm not sure. But you must feel it also if you're down here."

"Indeed. Have a seat," Venn motioned to another curve of wood.

Seth sat and crossed his legs, resting his back and folded wings against the smooth inner walls of the tree. "I dunno. On one hand the off weather pattern seems like a trivial thing, but coupled with all the unrest in the world——with ISIS beheading people in the Middle East and people protesting over police in the US——I think we need to pay close attention."

"I agree. The planet is digressing into a state of anarchy and I'd bet my right arm that the Dark Realm is behind it all," Venn proclaimed.

"No doubt."

"I think you'd better hang around," Venn suggested.

"Fine. You got a room to spare?" Seth asked, firing a glance from beneath heavy eyelids without lifting his head.

"No."

Seth shrugged. "Then I can't help you."

Venn chuckled, knowing full well he'd just gained a house guest. "It's hard to think back to when this guardianship began." He rested his head back and closed his eyes, trying to see that far into the past. "You know you could have given us a little more information when you set us on this task."

"What for? You figured it out."

"Huh. It took me forever to learn to control my shifting. The hawk being able to manipulate time and space, and the wolf's incredible strength. Shit, I was a mess in those days."

"You're still a mess," Seth said with exaggerated distain.

Venn straightened. "Hey, I didn't ask for this gig. You can head back up anytime."

Emma sympathized with anyone who had to make transatlantic flights on a regular basis. The trip from Paris to Atlanta's Hartsfield–Jackson airport had left her weary as a rag doll. Two hours later, she was still stifling yawns as she surveyed the snow-covered park where her mélange-metal statue would reside.

"I'm sorry. I shouldn't have made you stop here on the way from the airport. You must be exhausted." Grams tugged the zipper of her trendy black leather jacket higher before passing the leash attached to her little, aging Yorkshire terrier, Izzy, from one hand to the other. The pup scooted around her legs. "It was thoughtless of me. I'm just so excited."

Emma shrugged. "I'm fine," she assured her grandmother, then twisted to face the trunk of the enormous tree they stood beneath when the next yawn came. A whisper of energy coiled around her, heat seeming to seep out of the bark itself. She pursed her mouth and clasped her arms around her rib cage. As if the move offered any protection. Fatigue always made her paranoid. She even sometimes saw visions, though she didn't like to admit it, even to herself.

She sighed. No use in worrying about something she couldn't control, and she'd long since learned she wasn't in the driver's seat where her visions were concerned. Instead, she engaged in her most prevalent form of evasion, her art.

Nothing wrong with burying problems in a little work.

She studied the space again. Which metals would capture the hues of oyster shells in the sky? What subject would best fit the colors? Emma jotted down some mental notes for her next project. She watched the changing colors of dusk descend on the park as clouds loomed, back-lit in an eerie coppery shimmer. The diffused light made the snow appear almost warm, the rocks somehow spongy, and the trees . . . They were mystical.

Her apprehension escalated as the walkway in front of her blurred. Her knees grew weak.

No. Not this time.

She sucked in a deep breath and tensed, resisting. But she knew with sickening certainty that the vision was coming. There was no controlling it . . .

An arrow shaft protruded from her chest, and air wheezed through her stagnant lungs. In the wake of the brutal, radiating pain, time slowed. Her heart stopped.

Oh God.

An image of a huge gray wolf materialized, howling a cry of grief alongside her lifeless body, and it lingered, dimming slowly to a sepia shadow. Had she . . . died here?

Emma blinked, disoriented, as the brief manifestation faded, reality setting back in. Exhaling hard, she shifted her feet, peering down at her strappy, crystal-embellished, leopard-print sandals and seeking solid ground. Izzy licked at her toes where they peeked from her shoes, as if trying to console her as best he could. Her gaze swept up her own body, and she settled shaky fingers over her beating heart. No blood. No arrow. Definitely alive.

Still, the suffocating sensation of a collapsed lung remained, causing her stomach to churn. How she even knew what one felt like alarmed her.

Stop thinking about it.

With determined strength, Emma overcame the pervasive mental intrusion, forcing her attention back to the grossly neglected Georgia park where she stood trembling, to the place her sculpture would call home. She'd had these dreams and visions her whole life, and when she'd researched the phenomenon, she'd discovered they were each giving her a glimpse of one of her past lives. If one believed in that sort of thing. Which she did. But knowing that didn't make it any less disturbing.

Emma's breath swirled in a misty cloud as she focused on her surroundings. Cold, damp air patted her cheeks. The massive oak before her released a sad moan. Or was that just her active imagination at work? Whatever it was triggered a familiar warmth that spread into her limbs, and reminded her she possessed . . . talents beyond her visions. Heat radiated through her right arm, and she glanced down, opening her blazing hot fist to discover she'd inadvertently melted her grandmother's butterfly key fob beyond recognition.

Some *talents*. More like she'd been cursed.

With an unsteady sigh, she pushed her hair away from her face. Geez, her life hadn't changed one iota. Since she was a toddler, she'd been molding metal with her bare hands as if it were clay, both intentionally and accidentally. It was the latter that caused her grief. The episode with a neighborhood boy and his squished red Hot Wheels car came to mind. It always did. Her dad had been so angry with her.

"Are you okay?"

Her grandmother's question snapped her back to the present. Would Grams know if she lied? She'd discovered when she'd moved to

New York that the visions and dreams had lessened with the distance. She'd run all the way to Paris to avoid them. And they must have let go, too, because she hadn't thought of them for a long, long while.

"Sure. But I can't say the same for this." She dangled the key chain in the air.

Her grandmother gave a chuckle. "I should have nicknamed you Hot Hands."

Emma managed to summon a smile, but it faltered as her gaze shifted back to that tree. Its spindly canopy of branches seemed to reach out. The hair on her arms prickled. Something in the fractures of time yanked free and another ripple of unease washed over her.

Good and evil used this place as a playground. At the moment, evil acted the bully. She felt a bizarre tug-of-war for dominance, the power of it making her sway. *Leave. Me. Alone.*

─ell─

Pick up AWAKENING FIRE.

About Author

Larissa Emerald has always had a powerful creative streak whether it's altering sewing patterns, or the need to make some minor change in recipes, or frequently rearranging her home furnishings, she relishes those little walks on the wild side to offset her otherwise quite ordinary life. Her eclectic taste in books cover numerous genres, and she writes paranormal romance, and futuristic romantic thrillers. But no matter the genre or time period, she likes strong women dire situations who find the one man who will adore her beyond reason and give up everything for true love.

Larissa is happy to connect with her readers. Stop by and say hello: Website, Facebook,or send her an email: larissaemerald@gmail.com

Also By

Nocturne Falls Universe:

The Vampire Bounty Hunter's Unexpected CatchThe Shaman
Charms the Shifter

The Inspector Claims the Vampiress

The Dragon Falls for the Fairy Godmother

The Lion, the Witch, and the Secret Garden

Merry & Bright Anthology – The Witch's Snow Globe Wish

Winter Wonderland: A Christmas Quartet – Rockin' Around the
Cauldron